ESCAPE

Break For Freedom

GEORGE RENTON

authorHOUSE®

AuthorHouse™ UK
1663 Liberty Drive
Bloomington, IN 47403 USA
www.authorhouse.co.uk
Phone: UK TFN: 0800 0148641 (Toll Free inside the UK)
*   UK Local: (02) 0369 56322 (+44 20 3695 6322 from outside the UK)*

Published by AuthorHouse 01/19/2022

ISBN: 978-1-6655-9548-3 (sc)
ISBN: 978-1-6655-9547-6 (e)

Print information available on the last page.

This book is printed on acid-free paper.

Other titles by this author (published by AuthorHouseUK)
A COLLECTION OF NOVELLAS

CONTENTS

MAN OVERBOARD IN THE ENGLISH CHANNEL

A work of fiction set in the 1970s

ONE

The residents of Bournemouth's East Cliff awoke one summer morning, as they usually did, in an oasis of tranquillity. The hustle and bustle of Bournemouth's busy streets, despite being quite near, was far enough away for them to be undisturbed in the serenity of their leafy surroundings. The sun, although not fully risen, shimmered brightly heralding the start of a typical, fine south coast summer day. All was right with the world, as it seemed; apart from something that was different.

Those with bedrooms looking out onto Manor Road sniffed the air and thought they could detect a whiff of tobacco smoke. In contrast, those with a view of East Overcliff Drive and the sea could not only detect tobacco smoke but also see huge clouds of it coming towards them from somewhere in the middle of Poole Bay. Now and then the south easterly breeze caused the smoke to billow and swirl about revealing the hull and superstructure of a large cargo vessel at anchor in the bay south of Boscombe Pier. It was quite evidently on fire. A crowd of onlookers gathered on the East Overcliff Drive and the murmur of their voices was just audible on the balconies of the luxury apartments and hotels which line the East Cliff from Lansdowne to Boscombe

Chine. It was such an unusual event that neighbours in these elegant residences, who normally greeted each other with no more than a courteous nod, abandoned their staid behaviour and launched into animated conversation seeking the least snippet of information about what ship it was and why it was on fire.

The interest grew when one elderly gentleman announced that from his vantage point on the eleventh floor and with his telescope, he had made out the name of the ship on the stern and had caught a glimpse of its ensign. He said that the name was "Rosa --------" or something similar and that the ensign was none that he knew. Amongst the crowd, now spreading onto the immaculate lawns in front of the first class hotels, the consensus was that the name "Rosa -------" indicated that the ship was from somewhere in South America and judging by the unmistakable smell of tobacco smoke it was carrying a cargo of cigars. The speculation intensified when someone with binoculars who had been observing the scene from the East Cliff Funicular, where there was a better smoke free view, said that he had seen a customs cutter approach the vessel and come alongside.

A wag in the crowd jested :

"Is this tobacco for your own personal use, sir?"

Such an unusual event could not escape the attention of the media for very long and first to arrive on the cliff top was a reporter from the Bournemouth Echo. Other journalists and a TV camera crew from Southampton had to ease their way through traffic around Ringwood and did not reach the scene until much later in the morning. Meanwhile, the increasing throng of sightseers on the East Cliff was beginning to irritate the residents of the properties overlooking the sea and one by one they withdrew behind closed doors and slammed their windows shut in order to "keep the soft furnishings from reeking of tobacco smoke for weeks to come". Moreover, the burning ship had lost its novelty interest and by nature they were not gapers and gawpers; other pursuits claimed their attention.

By 11 AM the tide had turned and the breeze had softened to a whisper. The little smoke that could be seen rose almost vertically from the vessel making its hull and superstructure clearly distinguishable. There was a flurry of activity on board and some of the onlookers said they could see what appeared to be a naval vessel alongside and firemen on deck.

Once the fire had been extinguished and the comings and goings of the official launches visiting the cargo ship had taken on a predictable monotony, the crowd began to disperse. Their curiosity had not been satisfied but other occupations were more appealing : visiting Hengistbury Head and Mudeford Quay or simply sunbathing somewhere on Bournemouth's seven miles of golden sands. None of them had the least idea what story lay behind the arrival of the foreign ship in Poole Bay and its cargo of burning tobacco.

TWO

It was a dark moonless night with a thick fog hanging over the surface of the sea. The shadow of a ship slid through the calm waters, its fog horn rending the air with one long blast every two minutes. As if in reply, a shore based diaphone boomed out two blasts every 60 seconds. Unwilling to trust solely to radar, the ship's captain had doubled the lookouts. In the crows nest, on the bridge and in the bow, all eyes were focused up ahead; nobody was looking at the deck when the shadowy figure of a man emerged from a hatch leading to the chain locker. He made his way to the portside lifeboat and hoisted himself up to the level of its gunwale. There he slipped an arm under the tarpaulin boat cover and after groping about for a brief moment, withdrew a jerry can of water. He then lowered himself down and carefully placed it on the deck. Again he hoisted himself up and this time took out a pack of flares. Pausing to look around to see if he was being observed, he released an old style wooden raft from its mountings and dragged it across the deck to the port rail. The din coming from the ship's fog horn and the diaphone made any scraping noise of the raft on the deck wholly inaudible. Then he went to a locker and took out a coil of one-inch hemp rope and a pair of gauntlets. With one end of the rope securely attached to the wooden raft, he tied the other end to the rail with a slippery hitch, leaving a tail long enough to reach from the deck down to the sea. He slipped the tail end of the rope through the handles of the jerry can and tied it with a round turn and two half hitches. Then taking a deep breath as if to prepare for some great exertion, he lifted the raft over the rail, held it in position and taking another deep breath eased it as gently as he could down the side of the vessel into the water. He waited for it to steady before lowering the jerry can of water on to it. The deafening boom of the fog horns covered any noise that he made. After one last glance to check that everything was ready, it was time to go. Tucking the flares and the gauntlets under his tunic and drawing the tunic belt tight around his waist, he stepped over the rail and slithered down the rope on to the wooden raft. Making sure that he really had brought the water and the flares with him and that he still had some glucose lozenges in his pocket, he gave a tug on the free end of the slippery hitch. The rope came tumbling down on to the raft. Then with a foot on the side of the ship, he pushed himself away from the hull and watched as it glided slowly past him. The ship was hardly making way through the water and it took more than a minute before the huge bulk of the stern loomed above him revealing for a brief moment the name of the ship and its port of registration. Then it disappeared into the fog and the night, its wash barely rocking the little raft. His meticulously conceived plan had succeeded; he was adrift in the English Channel and was sure that he had not been observed leaving the ship by any of his shipmates. They would continue to think that he had been swept overboard during the storm.

In two hours the sun would rise and the fog would clear. By that time he would be well astern of the ship. What if later in the day somebody were to notice that the raft was missing and wonder if there was a link between the missing raft and the missing man? He gave thought to this possibility and decided that most likely he had already been reported in the ship's log as lost overboard during a damage control emergency and that nobody would think to change that version of events. This is what he wanted. Perhaps the absence of the wooden raft would be explained by it having been washed overboard when the ship listed during the storm; the crew being too preoccupied with other matters failed to notice. Now alone, and five miles from the nearest land, he reflected on what he had done and remained convinced that it was his best option. Better by far to perish at sea than endure the fate that awaited him back in his homeport. He felt with his hand for the flares tucked under his tunic and was reassured by their presence. Then, marshalling his thoughts, he took the rope, still made fast to the raft and tied the free end around his waist in a bowline. Should he fall asleep and be tipped off the crude wooden platform by a choppy sea, he would still be attached to it. However, the risk of rough seas was remote. When last on the bridge, a glance at the most recent weather chart had shown him that once the storm had abated and the ship had passed Ushant they would encounter fog all along the coast of Brittany. This would be followed by clear skies and light breezes lasting for days due to a slow moving anticyclone situated somewhere to the west of the English Channel out in the Atlantic. Surely in this shipping lane some lookout on the bridge of a passing ship would see his raft and he would be rescued long before the weather worsened. For the time being it was vital to focus all his attention on surviving till the sun came up.

There was a risk that in this traffic separation zone, in fog and at night, another ship proceeding along the same route as his own would simply not see him and run him down. The chances of being hit by a big ship and surviving, even at slow speeds, were slender. However, there was something that could be done to prevent a run-down. The fog horn and the engines of an approaching ship would alert him to the danger and he could fire a white flare, commonly known as a *ship-scarer*. Its bright light would surely illuminate the bridge of the ship and unless those on watch were dozing, he would be rescued. He knew that he did not have to wait long for the dawn; together with other essential details, he had memorised the times of sunrise and sunset.

⁂

Eventually the sun came up and immediately started to warm his chilly body. As the sky grew lighter, the fog thinned and in less than an hour the visibility had noticeably improved. Soon, he hoped, he would be able to see some mark on the coast and get his bearings. When planning his escape he had studied the admiralty charts, tide tables and tidal atlas and had a good idea of when and which way the tides would sweep him.

He scanned the horizon, first on his knees and then standing up. With a height of eye some six feet above the surface of the sea, his horizon was approximately three miles whilst the geographical range of the Casquets Lighthouse was 28 miles. Added together that made 31 miles; more than enough for the three towers on this rocky outcrop to the northwest of Alderney to be visible from where he knew himself to be. He was in audible range of the Casquets diaphone and so could not be far off. At present there was still too much mist to see more than two or so miles.

Exhausted by his exertions and the nervous tension involved in getting off the ship and onto the raft, he fell asleep. When he awoke the first thing he became aware of was the diaphone; he could no longer hear it. This meant that the fog had cleared. Getting to his knees, he quickly assessed which way his shadow was pointing and turned his gaze to where he expected to see what he knew looked like the three funnels of a World War 1 battleship. Reassuringly the three towers of the Casquets Lighthouse were there on the horizon gleaming in the bright early morning sunshine.

A quick calculation told him that the tide would soon be sweeping eastwards towards the northernmost Channel Island, Alderney. This was inevitable and might hasten his rescue. It was time to see if an idea he had had was workable. He took the gauntlets from inside his tunic and put them on. They fitted well enough. Then plunging a gauntleted hand into the water, he began to paddle and was gratified to see that he could steer the raft, albeit rather clumsily. If the need arose he might be able to steer away from jagged rocks and on to a beach.

Feeling more sure about the outcome of his adventure, his mind began to wander over the events of the past few hours and then deeper into the past.

Erica was a pretty girl although not overtly sexy and certainly not the sort that wanted to attract lots of men. She was demure but not shy, intelligent and well read but not aloof. They had become acquainted two years previously when on holiday. Since then they had written to each other regularly but because of the circumstances that separated them, the correspondence had had to be cloaked in secrecy. What ingenuity they showed in finding ways of ensuring that their innocent letters got through all the barriers to communication. Although worthy of a super-spy, this ingenuity was not motivated by the thrill of beating the system and getting the better of a tyrannical bureaucracy. During the three weeks they had spent together a genuine affection had developed between them. They were destined for each other.

Heidi, his wife in name only, was much too self centred and craved constant attention from men, especially men in positions of power. He was certain she was unfaithful to him and worse still, had spied on him in order to win favour and get a well paid promotion. At first tormented by her infidelity when he was at sea, he came to appreciate the long weeks spent away from her. He had not married thinking that he would want to get a divorce within less than five years, but there was no denying it: he would be glad to be rid of her. Deep down he acknowledged that he had been foolish. For professional reasons he needed to marry and had not shown good sense in his choice of fiancee. Each time he returned from sea, it became more and more apparent that behind her effervescent displays of affection lay a scheming social climber who saw him as a mere stepping stone to something she knew he could never provide. He had been bewitched by her. Erica was everything Heidi was not and if all went according to plan he would soon be able to join her.

THREE

In Braye Harbour, on the Isle of Alderney, there was a bustle of activity aboard the Lotus Flower. The crew of this sixty-foot ketch were preparing for sea; squaring away and stowing all lose items. Meanwhile, skipper Steve was telling them what to expect during the crossing to Dartmouth.

"We've got settled weather for our passage back to Blighty. The seas will slight and the wind from the south-west, force two, perhaps three. The fog is clearing and the visibility should be good."

With the headsail and main set and the engine running in neutral, the yacht slipped from its moorings and slowly got underway steering north-east-by-north. Still in the lee of the breakwater, its sails more flogging than filling, it glided forward as if propelled by some magic force. Suddenly, a gust made the headsail and main billow, the yacht heeled slightly and began to cleave a path through the greeny-blue sea. Soon the end of the breakwater lay astern and with Quenard Lighthouse off the starboard beam, skipper Steve turned the engine off and asked two of his crew to hoist the mizzen. Then, setting a course somewhat west of north, they began their passage across the English Channel.

Soon Alderney was a mere smudge on the horizon and

the crew were already in watches; red, white and blue, each doing three hours steering and lookout followed by six hours off, sleeping and/or sun bathing. The deck was in the hands of blue watch with Dave at the wheel. Steve had gone below and was in the doghouse writing in the bosun's book a list of repairs and sundry maintenance to be carried out whilst alongside in Dartmouth. His reflections on what was essential and what might be postponed were interrupted by a call from John, the lookout.

"Skipper, I can see somehing up ahead. There, off the port bow. It's gone now. For brief moment it looked like a man raising and lowering his arms."

Steve reached for his binoculars and took them out of their rack. He was about to put a foot on the ladder leading topsides when he heard his crew say :

"Skipper, now he's fired a red flare. Look."

With one bound Steve was on deck. The flare was still burning and through the binoculars he saw a man on what looked like a raft.

"OK, everybody, that is a distress signal. We've practised MOB, (man-overboard recovery) before. Today, it's for real. You know what to do. Dave, you stay at the wheel and John, you control the main sheet. Remember, don't pull it through the pulleys. Just grab the whole sheaf and tug it just enough to fill the sail. We'll pick him up on the port side. Now, ease the sheets and let fly. Dave, turn and bring us onto a beam reach with the raft under our port bow. John, give a tug on the main sheet, just enough to ease us forward."

Slowly and steadily the yacht came alongside the raft. Skipper Steve tied a bowline in a soft rope and threw it to the man who slipped it over his head and under his armpits.

Between them, passing the rope from one to another along the port rail, the crew manoeuvred the man on his raft to the boarding ladder aft, saw him steady himself and then put a foot on the first rung, again steady himself and climb aboard.

"Welcome aboard" said Steve. "Take him below, Jenny and see if he's hypothermic. Well done everybody. OK. Let's get back on course. I think it's time for a cuppa. Will somebody not on watch see to that. You'll have to switch the gas back on."

Steve joined Jenny, an NHS A&E nurse in the saloon below decks. They looked at the man. He was in his late twenties or early thirties. He was dressed in a dark blue, heavy cotton tunic and trousers. On his feet he wore black deck shoes. Considering he had just come off a raft, all these items of clothing were remarkably dry. This was all the more surprising given that he must have been on the raft several days judging by the growth of beard he had. She said to the man in a tone which combined professional efficiency and care for her patients:

"We want to know if you are alright. Will you let me examine you. I am a nurse."

He looked confused and replied in English but with a strong accent :

"What? I OK? No - Yes? I OK."

Jenny reached out a hand and took the man's pulse. He acquiesced. His heart beat was normal and his skin was not excessively cold to the touch.

She said "I don't think you are hypothermic. You are not a medical emergency. Now we are going to have a coffee. Would you like some?"

"Koffee. Yes. I trink Koffee. OK.."

"By the way, I'm Jenny and this is Steve. What is your name?"

"Me? Mine Name - Oscar."

Skipper Steve was reassured that the MOB was none the worse for having been adrift on a raft for several days, as it seemed to him. There was no medical emergency. Nevertheless he did have cause for concern. The man did not speak much English and so was not British. He appeared to be dressed in some sort of a seaman's uniform and it was not obvious how he came to be on a raft adrift in the English Channel.

These thoughts made him remember the raft which in the flurry of activity attending to the MOB, he had forgotten. Now with matters under control he went up into to the cockpit and looked about him. The raft was bobbing up and down two hundred yards away. He began to wonder what he should have done with it. Taking it in tow was not an option; it would be a hazard and the insurance specifically excluded towing dinghies offshore and very likely rafts too. The only course of action was to abandon it. He had only seen it close-up for a minute or two but he had the clear impression that it was made of wood and had at one time been painted red and white. He also wondered what else had been left on the raft apart from a jerry can of water and another item. They would surely have provided clues as to the identity and origins of their shipwrecked sailor.

Another question came into his mind; was this mystery man a danger to his crew and to himself and was his real name Oscar? In the international code of signals, Oscar represents the letter "O" and stands for man-overboard.

After a few moments thought, he concluded that the man did not appear to be dangerous and his crew were all young and fit people well able to take care of themselves. In any case what would a yacht pirate be doing on a raft miles off land. As a way of hijacking a yacht, it would be unjustifiably hazardous, too dependent on chance and so unlikely to succeed. These thoughts aside, they were inward bound and had an extra passenger who would have to be declared to the authorities. Should he alert the emergency services on the RT he wondered. No, he told himself. There was no emergency. Then another worrying thought came into his mind. There had been no announcement on the RT of an MOB in the Channel. Had Oscar been cast adrift by his shipmates in the hope that he would perish? If so, he did not want Lotus Flower to be in any way involved with desperados who clearly had no respect for human life or the law of the sea. Radio silence was the safest course.

Having debated these matters in his mind it was time to make a crew announcement.

"Lend an ear everybody. You all performed well during the man-overboard recovery. The drills have paid off. Good for you. Now, this is the position. We are still passage making to Dartmouth. We have an extra passenger but that does not mean that we have to change our passage plans. We have a duty as mariners to give what assistance we can to other mariners and we have done that more than adequately. We will deliver our shipwrecked sailor to the authorities in Dartmouth. I have decided that there is no need to alert the emergency rescue services, the RNLI etc because the man is unharmed and safe on board with us. His chances of survival are as good as ours. To summon help that we do not need would delay us. I am at all times very conscious that you've all got jobs to go to and so want to get back home. So, we maintain our course and speed."

Then turning to Oscar, the shipwrecked sailor, Steve said

"Come and have a look at the chart. This is where we are going—Dartmouth" he said pointing to Start Point and the River Dart.

Oscar was delighted to learn that the yacht was bound for Dartmouth and smiled broadly in approval. Ships of our fleet never put into the River Dart and are too big for Brixham, he mused. After a quick calculation he decided that at a speed of around three knots the yacht and his rescuers would arrive in Dartmouth sometime the next day in the late hours of the morning. By that time my ship will be through the Straits of Dover, he said to himself.

FOUR

⚭

Fifteen days previously, in Havana, Cuba, on board the freighter Rosa Luxemburg, a meeting took place in the captain's day cabin. Seated around the table were the captain, the chief engineer and the political officer.

The political officer, notionally subordinate to the captain and the chief engineer, seemed to be exercising his authority and this much to the displeasure of the other two.

"We must be disciplined and adhere to the schedule. Therefore, we must leave harbour tomorrow in order to reach our home port by the date set out in the plan. We do not want to be in default."

The chief engineer nodded in agreement and said:

"Of course fulfilling the plan is our objective. But, essential maintenance must be carried out before we put to sea. The spares requested will arrive tomorrow or the day after and the repairs will take about ten hours, maybe less."

"Are all the generators out of action? What's wrong with them? Surely, they'll last another two weeks or so until we reach our home port. That's the best place for repairs, not alongside in a foreign port. It's the first time I've ever heard of generators needing so much maintenance."

"It's not only the generators. There's a bearing which needs attention."

"Are you waiting for spares to fix a bearing? What other excuses do you have for the delay?"

At this point the captain intervened:

"I will not take this ship to sea unless I am sure she is fit for sea. I have my responsibilities, not least to the crew. However, a compromise must be found between safety and the schedule. Would it be possible to get underway and do some of the most essential jobs while at sea?"

"Doing that sort of work on the generators at sea is far from ideal. What is more, no responsible engineer would choose to strip down No 4 in heavy weather and we can't be sure what sort of weather we're going to get. Can we? What's more, we may need to make some parts in the workshop. And whilst I think of it, there's the dodgy bearing. It's been running too hot for my liking. We'll have to strip it down sometime and that means stopping the engines. I don't know what's wrong. It is most likely the oil feed. In which case it's not a long job, but it's best done alongside."

"We are not an isolated unit. We are part of a carefully elaborated plan involving berthing, unloading and onward transport. If we fail to arrive in port on schedule, the workings of the port, the haulage system and production at the factories awaiting our cargo will be disrupted. We've already failed once this year and our chances of winning a prize for efficiency will be nil."

There ensued a long pause; all three sat motionless in total silence, not looking at each other. To an outsider observing the proceedings, it would have seemed like a tableau from the waxworks. The clock on the bulkhead ticked the seconds and minutes away. After nearly three minutes, it was the captain who spoke first:

"We go tomorrow."

"I am relieved to hear it" said the political officer. Then anxious to emphasise that the discussion was over and that he would entertain no further objections, he left the captain's day cabin in great haste. Had he remained in the presence of his two shipmates he might have noticed them exchange a smile indicating satisfaction at having won the argument. They had got the better of the young fire-brand; he needed to be reminded that he was a subordinate.

As teenagers, Fritz Mueller and Otto Hengerer were destined for a life in Germany's merchant marine. It was as cadets in the late 1930s that they first became acquainted. When World War Two broke out they had not completed their training, nonetheless, eager to serve the Fatherland, they joined the Kriegsmarine and by chance both served on the Tirpitz. This big battleship, sister to the Bismarck, hardly ventured out, spending most of the war sheltering in a Norwegian Fjord. Despite this, it remained a threat to British shipping and in consequence was the target for several daring raids by the Royal Navy and the Royal Air Force. Miraculously Fritz and Otto survived these attacks and the ultimate destruction of the ship.

During their service on the Tirpitz neither of them exhibited any enthusiasm for Nazism, a possible explanation for their not being promoted. After the war, this lack of enthusiasm for Nazism ripened into a genuine loathing for Hitler and the Third Reich. Still in their mid-twenties they settled back into civilian life in the Pomeranian coastal towns on the Baltic where they had been raised. Finishing their training in the Ostseehandelsmarineschule and resuming their careers as merchant seamen was the obvious course of action. Being totally absorbed by their nautical studies, neither of them had the leisure or the foresight to enquire deeply into the full significance of the ideological rift that was developing between the Allies and how it would lead to Germany being divided. By virtue of having a home address on the communist side of the "iron curtain" they were destined to become citizens of East Germany. A circumstance which did not cause them much anxiety given their lingering loathing of Nazism and the firm belief that communism was a progressive political force and preferable to exploitative capitalism.

Fritz Mueller became a deck officer and Otto Hengerer a ship's engineer. In post-war East Germany, they soon found employment in the Ostseehandelschiffsbetrieb. Rostock, their home port, was to become East Germany's principal "ocean" port.

FIVE

Four days out, during the forenoon watch, the chief engineer appeared on the bridge and informed the captain that a bearing was overheating due to a defective oil feed pump. It would need to be stripped down and for that it would be best and quicker to stop both engines. A minimum of four hours, perhaps even six, would be needed to carry out the work. Captain Mueller stared at the chief engineer and somewhat reluctantly gave the order to "STOP BOTH". The Rosa Luxemburg slowly lost way and came to a halt. However, she was not motionless; a westerly swell caused her to sway through an arc of forty degrees which even in the depths of the engine room was appreciable and not ideal for carrying out maintenance. The captain sent an apprentice deck hand to summon the political officer. Let him come to me here on the bridge, he said to himself. It was time for him to confront reality and recognise that political motivation cannot overcome technical problems. An engine overhaul takes the time necessary for an engine overhaul. The captain, the chief engineer and the crew were all professional seamen and did not need "motivating" by a young upstart who thought that quoting party doctrine would compensate for a lack of experience and that simply repeating "Where there's a will there's a way" can solve all problems.

On board the Rosa Luxemburg, most incoming signals were in plain text; others with commercially sensitive information were in code. Yet others were triple-encoded and only decipherable by Schneider, the political officer who kept the code books in his cabin, in a safe to which he alone had the key. Not even the captain could decipher them. However such signals were very rare, indeed exceptional.

Two days after the ship had got underway again following the repairs to the oil feed pump, a triple-encoded signal was received. Before putting it in the political officer's pigeon hole, the radio operator showed it to 2cnd officer Schulz. Neither Schulz nor the radio operator could read the signal but the fact that it had been sent gave them both cause for thought; especially Schulz. He wondered why it had been sent triple-encoded and what it said that needed to be kept from everybody else. He had the distinct feeling that it might concern him and he began to surreptitiously observe Schneider in order to detect some clue as to whether the signal had been about him. If he was the subject of the signal, he felt sure he knew why. His secret correspondence had been discovered. Reading between the lines he deduced that this was to be his last trip and that the secret police wanted to interview him. He would most likely be arrested on his return to Rostock, the ship's home port. Nonetheless, he could not reproach himself with having been careless.

Whilst in La Havana, as on all other occasions when ashore, 2cnd officer Schulz strolled around the city streets, aimlessly as it might have seemed to a casual observer. This was quite deliberate; it was intended to conceal the fact that he was a man with a distinct purpose. At every street crossing he turned to see if he was being followed. At major junctions, he mingled with the other pedestrians waiting to cross the road and when they all moved forward, instead of crossing with the crowd, he turned sharply into side streets hoping to confuse anybody tailing him. After half an hour of twisting and turning, feeling sure that he had not been followed, he finally arrived at his destination: the central post office.

He saw a free counter clerk sitting behind a grill. He approached her:

"Per favor, unas sellas para Bundes Republik Aleman."

Content that she appeared to understand his Spanish but disconcerted that he did not understand the reply, he delved into his pocket, pulled out some bank notes together with a few coins and put them on the counter in front of her.

The young woman smiled indulgently at him, sorted through the money laid before her, took what she needed and pushed the rest back to him. She stuck the stamps on the postcard, glanced at the writing on it and saw that it was addressed to somebody called Erica with an unpronounceable surname, in a place called Hamburg. Concluding that Schulz was a visitor and that Erica was his girl friend she whispered something which he did not understand and gave him a warm smile.

Schulz waited long enough to see her slip the post card into a mail sack. Then he turned around very slowly and studied the faces of the people behind him. There was not one familiar face amongst them. He breathed a sigh of relief. The last time he had posted a card to Erica, he recognised a face in the crowd standing behind him in the post office. It was the assistant ship's cook and aide to the political officer. He pretended not to see her but felt sure she had seen him mailing a post card. Everybody on board knew that she was a Stasi informer and that she reported everything she saw and heard.

Political officer Schneider's reply to the triple-encoded signal was not long in coming. The radio operator did not keep this fact to himself. First, he very discreetly informed his old friend Schulz that Schneider had sent a triple-encoded signal back to their base on the Baltic Sea. He then passed the information on to the captain and chief engineer. Neither Schulz, nor the captain and chief engineer, were surprised to learn that a reply had been sent, only the length of it gave them cause for thought. It was 2500 letters long, all sent in groups of five so that no word would be distinguishable by its length.

Schulz was extremely anxious but managed to conceal his anxiety about the length of the message sent back to their base. He knew this was not routine, not even for Schneider. He began to face up to the possibility that after docking in their home port he would be arrested and then dismissed from his post as second officer, *de-qualified*, stripped of his rank and never allowed to work at sea again or even in any occupation which might enable him to have contact with the outside world.

For their part, the captain and chief engineer were also perplexed by the length of the signal sent triple-encoded. They held an urgent meeting, but not in the captain's cabin. They arranged to meet, as if by chance, on the foredeck where they could not be overheard. They had good cause to be cautious. Political officer Schneider was orphaned towards the end of the second world war and had been taken in by the *Partei*. It was in one of their orphanages that he had been brought up. Such individuals were fiercely loyal to the party and could be utterly ruthless in the fulfilment of their duty. Schneider was a Stasi Mitarbeiter.

The East German secret police, the Stasi, kept files on one third of the population of their country, that is more than 5 million citizens. Erich Mielke, the Stasi director, was assisted in his task of spying on his own people by 90 thousand full time agents and another 170 thousand unofficial collaborators. Young people, eager to please, were told that by informing they would help to prevent the chaos that enemies of the State wished to create in order to destroy their socialist republic and replace it with a harsh capitalist regime in which they would be little better than slaves.

The deputy minister in charge of trade with capitalist countries was a committed communist who saw every contact with the outside world as an opportunity to project an image of a perfect Marxist-Leninist, socialist society, disciplined, loyal and hard working. To some extent he succeeded; customs officers in foreign ports, when extremely busy, would content themselves with giving East German ships no more than a token inspection, convinced that the strict discipline which prevailed would allow no opportunities for smugglers.

SIX

After ten days at sea and with the vast expanse of the Atlantic astern, the Rosa Luxemburg was about to enter the Western Approaches. For two days the weather had been stormy, with rain lashing down and the wind gusting eight to nine. Unlike the long Atlantic waves, the steeper seas of the Western Approaches made the Rosa Luxemburg pitch and roll. Ahead lay the Ushant traffic separation zone, a sea lane some three miles wide lying to the north-west of Ushant, an island off the French coast. All vessels entering the English Channel were required to proceed inward and up-channel within the bounds of this zone.

Captain Mueller was awakened by the alarm bell ringing. His hand stretched out to the voice pipe above his head :

"Report! What is the problem? Is there a fire?"

"No comrade captain" came the answer from the bridge. "The chief reports water sloshing about in the bilges and even the gratings in the engine room are awash."

"Water? How much water? How did it get there?"

"We're paddling about here and the chief says he has no idea where it is coming from. The boatswain and third officer have roused the off-watch crew and are now organising a stem-to-stern below-decks inspection of all the rivets."

"If there were a gash due to blown rivets somebody down below would surely have heard a loud report, even in these heavy seas it would sound like a cannon being fired."

"Yes, comrade captain. The chief said something like that too. So he's gone to inspect the stuffing box. It could be leaking water. She's been pitching a lot and the screw has been racing. This may have done some damage."

Mueller swivelled round and put his feet on the deck below his bunk. Still in his pyjamas, he hastily pulled on his uniform trousers and eased a heavy woollen pullover over his head. Slipping his feet into his sea boots, he grabbed his sou'wester and in two strides was out in the corridor and on his way to the bridge.

The storm had abated but huge waves were still lashing the decks. The sky was dark and menacing and Mueller could only make out shadows as he climbed up to the bridge. Once in the command centre, he ordered "SLOW AHEAD". It was essential to maintain steerage way but also to reduce the speed of the ship so as to minimise the inflow of any water that might be entering the vessel through a gash in the side.

Meanwhile, third officer Schmidt had mobilised a team of deck hands to manoeuvre a huge canvas along the port side of the ship to search for a gash in the hull through which the water could be leaking. If there was a leak, the pressure of sea water pouring through the gash would drive the canvas hard against the hull, so plugging the leak and blocking the further inrush of water. They were all attached to a lifeline which ran fore and aft in order to prevent them being washed overboard. It was difficult work in the dark with the deck pitching and rolling under their feet.

As he stood on the bridge awaiting reports about a possible gash in the hull, the captain watched the damage control team on deck. It was dark and although he could not be sure, it seemed to him that the second officer did not appear to be taking command of the exercise. Schulz should also be looking for the leak and not leave it all to the third officer and the boatswain.

A huge sea which seemed to come from nowhere made the ship heel causing all those on-deck to lose their footing. Only the fore and aft lifeline prevented them from being pitched overboard. Then after two massive cascades of water had crashed down on the deck, the boatswain, wiping the stinging salt water from his eyes, turned his head away to avoid a third deluge and just happened to see something that alarmed him. The forward hatch was open for some three metres on the weather side and every time a huge wave swept over the deck masses of water rushed into the opening and down into the bilges. How long it had been open like that he could not imagine. Had it been properly fastened when the ship prepared for sea or was there a saboteur amongst the crew? Unlikely, he told himself. Who would so recklessly endanger the ship and the lives of all on board? Whatever the explanation, there was now so much water in the bilges that it was causing the ship to roll more heavily each time a wave struck the hull. It had begun to flood the engine room. Nonetheless, it was a relief to know that the likelihood of there being a gash in the hull could be eliminated; the water was entering the ship through an open hatch.

All these thoughts ran through the boatswain's mind

in a fraction of a second as he took immediate steps to close the hatch. On closer inspection he saw that the tarpaulins had been peeled back and were flogging in wind but that the portable beams were still intact. Only the hatch boards were missing and nowhere to be seen on deck. Other hatch boards were found and slotted in. After which the tarpaulins were battened down with steel battens and wooden wedges. All these closing procedures were supervised by third officer Schmidt who then reported to the captain on the bridge that the likely cause of water in the engine room was an open hatch and that he had seen it properly closed.

Minutes later came the reassuring news that the level of water in the engine room had started to fall. This was a relief to all. The chief engineer had made it known that not only generator number four but also one of the ship's pumps needed servicing. Everybody was aware that if both were to fail, the other generators and pumps, even running at full capacity, might not be able to cope with the amount of water in the bilges.

The emergency past, the captain began to think about what had occurred. He wanted to know why it was third officer Schmidt and not second officer Schulz who had supervised the closing of the hatch. He ordered Schulz to come to the bridge to explain why, when the ship was in danger, he was absent from his post. Such dereliction of duty was a serious matter. Schulz did not respond to calls on his voice pipe and so the captain sent apprentice deck-hand Kellerman to tell him to come to the bridge. Minutes later Kellerman appeared and informed the captain that Schulz was not in his cabin nor anywhere to be seen in the officers' quarters.

The captain furrowed his brow and ordered the ship to be searched. Despite being exhausted after the damage control emergency, all off duty hands were roused and told to find second officer Schulz. Reports came in from all parts below decks that Schulz was nowhere to be found.

The captain ordered them to look again. Where was Schulz he asked himself. The first officer and three crew members were in the sick bay incapacitated with gastro-enteritis together with an apprentice deck hand who had suffered a sprained ankle. Now, it looked highly likely that the second officer had been swept overboard. Repeated searches failed to find Schulz. With sadness for the loss of a shipmate and concern for his professional standing, the captain made the appropriate entry in the ship's log.

The next day an enquiry was held. Officially it was the captain who presided but in reality, political officer Schneider ran the proceedings. One by one, all on board were interrogated by him about where they were and what they were doing and who might have seen them doing it. The political officer was very thorough. Nonetheless, no explanation was found for the open hatch which had jeopardised the lives of all on board nor for the loss of the second officer presumably swept away by the sea during the storm.

An inspection of the forward hold revealed that a cargo of rum in casks appeared not to have suffered water damage and that the whole space was drying out. Tobacco and cane sugar in the other holds showed no signs of having been touched by the ingress of sea water.

SEVEN

❧

The sun had already set as the Rosa Luxemburg entered the traffic separation zone off the Casquets. All vessels were required to maintain their course and speed within a lane three miles wide in order to avoid collision. The visibility was poor due to it being a dark moonless night, made worse by a thick fog which hung over the surface of the sea. Slow ahead and double lookouts was the order from the bridge. Every two minutes the boom of the ship's fog horn rent the air, warning other vessels of its presence. Throughout the night the ship eased its way slowly forward. As the sun came up the fog began to clear, the visibility improved and the ship increased speed. Nobody had seen the second officer slip overboard onto a raft. They all believed that he had been swept away by a huge wave during the storm.

It was the boatswain who alerted the bridge that an aroma of burning tobacco had begun to pervade the air below decks. At first he had ignored it, thinking that it was due to excessive smoking in the crew's quarters. However, later, when it had grown too heavy to be dismissed as cigarette smoke, he realised that only one explanation was likely: there must be a fire in number four hold where bales of tobacco were stowed. An experienced seaman, who did not believe in jinxes, the boatswain wrestled with his suspicions that there was a saboteur on board. The mid-Atlantic overhaul of an oil feed pump, the open hatch cover on number one hold, the second officer lost overboard and a possible fire in number four hold, all amounted to a series of mishaps the like of which in his thirty years at sea he had never known before. He began to wonder what else could occur to endanger their lives.

Reports came to the bridge from the third officer that indeed tobacco was smouldering in number four hold and that it would be impossible to prevent a full conflagration without dowsing the bales of tobacco with water; chemical extinguishers would not be sufficient. The below-decks access to the hold was through a small door in the bulkhead. Sadly, this door was much too narrow to allow for the full deployment of the hoses. If the first attempts to quench the fire were unsuccessful there would be no alternative but to open the hatch covers and drench the cargo with cascades of water from all on deck fire appliances. However, this course of action was not risk free; opening the hatch covers would allow air to enter the hold and turn the smouldering tobacco into a blaze.

Hardly had the full impact of this report been assessed when the chief engineer appeared on the bridge to inform the captain that number four generator had broken down. The implication of this news was apparent to all. Nonetheless, the chief engineer explained the fine detail of the situation in a deliberate and unhurried fashion. All those present heard clearly what he said and were in no doubt that with only three functioning generators to power fire fighting appliances, all non-essential electrical systems, including below-deck ventilation and lighting, would have to be shut down. There would only be enough power for communications and other requirements necessary for the ship to remain under command. Without below-deck ventilation and lighting the crew would be in danger of choking from smoke inhalation not to mention injury when stumbling about in the dark. Having delivered his grim message to the captain and crew, the chief engineer left the bridge. Only those who were truly observant might just have caught the faintest twitch of a facial muscle that passed between the two senior officers.

Captain Mueller did not hesitate. He ordered "STOP BOTH" on the engine room telegraph. As the ship began to lose way, the radio operator was ordered to inform the French authorities that there was a fire on board the Rosa Luxemburg and that all off duty crew were being evacuated into lifeboats. He was also ordered to send a short coded signal to the Schiffsbetrieb HQ in Rostock on the Baltic informing the desk bound managers that the Rosa Luxemburg was on fire and that the captain had ordered "ABANDON SHIP".

Slowly the vessel came to a standstill twenty nautical miles NE of Cap de la Hague off the French coast. The weather was warm with only a slight breeze to ripple an almost calm sea. If abandon ship is inevitable, it is best done in daylight, in calm seas and warm weather.

Captain Mueller was quite deliberate in determining the order of evacuation and in stipulating which members of the crew were to leave the ship. Only the third officer, the deckhands fighting the fire, a skeleton crew in the engine room, the radio operator and one lookout on the bridge were to remain on board with him. One of the lifeboats on the port side was not to be lowered into the water. If the fire could not be extinguished, those who stayed behind would need it to leave the ship.

Captain Mueller then issued orders that the five patients in the sick bay should be given priority and put in the first lifeboat ahead of all the others. Four of them were still weak from gastro-enteritis and the apprentice deck-hand was only able to hobble about on his sprained ankle. They would all need help to get off the ship. The boatswain, unwilling to leave, was given a direct order to take command of the lifeboat with the five crew members from the sick bay. He was a reliable seaman with long years of experience on sailing barges and the captain assured him that he could best serve his shipmates in the lifeboat with the sick bay patients.

At this point Schneider, the political officer appeared on the bridge. He was a non-smoker, who preferred serving on ships because the clean sea air did not trigger his asthma, a worsening medical condition which he had managed to conceal from the Schiffsbetrieb doctors during his last medical. His eyes were red and he was coughing and spluttering due to smoke inhalation. At every intake of breath he wheezed as if he were about to choke. Mueller looked at him, saw his pitiable state and ordered him to take to a lifeboat. Schneider raised no protest; he welcomed the chance to escape the smoke.

A few minutes later the political officer was in a lifeboat, being rowed clear of the ship. For a brief moment the captain felt a sensation of relief come over him. It was as if a dream were coming true : being rid of Schneider. Then, gathering his thoughts, Mueller ordered the radio operator to inform the French authorities that there were sick crew members taking to the lifeboats and to request medical assistance. This SOS was acknowledged and the SNSM French rescue service alerted. The sea was calm and the visibility good. It was risk free; they would all be rescued. As it happened most of the crew believed that there was a jinx on the ship and so when ordered to take to the boats they did not dawdle. Reassured about the safety of his crew, most of whom were in lifeboats, the captain was then free to concentrate on more urgent matters.

The chief engineer, twenty minutes after having returned to his engine room, announced that generator number four was again operational. Meanwhile, the third officer having marshalled the fire fighters decided that the hatch covers on number four hold would have to be removed if the fire was to be extinguished. Fighting the fire through a bulkhead door was no longer an option. He sought approval from the captain which was readily given. Once the hatch covers had been removed, the smouldering fire became a blaze sending smoke high up into the sky.

Guided by the smoke billowing high into the air the French rescue service was quick to arrive on the scene. First a helicopter to ferry the sick bay patients to hospital on shore and then powerful launches to take the ship's lifeboats in tow. The captain watched from the bridge as most of his crew disappeared over the horizon and out of sight.

Half an hour later, the third officer reported that the fire in hold number four was under control. To achieve this much of the cargo of leaf tobacco in the lower hold had been drenched with cascades of water taken from the deck hydrants. The emergency was over but the smouldering tobacco still needed to be dampened down because it could flare up again and spread to the cases of cigars in the upper hold.

On hearing this the captain turned to the bridge telegraph and rung down to the engine room "AHEAD BOTH". The Rosa Luxemburg sprang into life, the engines throbbed and the bow began to cut a clear path through the calm waters. The course was due north. Soon the faint smudge fine on the starboard bow became firmer and more clearly identifiable as St Catherine's Point, the southernmost tip of the Isle of Wight.

On the chart table was a chart of Poole Bay, from the Needles to Anvil Point. Mueller studied it carefully. He remembered from his sail training days before the Second World War how they had visited Poole Harbour and practised manoeuvres with other sail training schooners in the waters from Hengistbury Head to Sandbanks. Somewhere in Poole Bay to the South-East of Boscombe Pier would be an ideal place to anchor the Rosa Luxemburg.

EIGHT

A defining feature of communism was the *command economy,* accompanied by a harsh suppression of *the market.* The production and processing of raw materials, the manufacture of components and their assembly into finished goods, indeed all economic activity was determined by state planning. There were no entrepreneurs free to create a business in order to respond to a growing demand. An unintended consequence of this restriction of free choice was an inadequacy of supplies for industrial enterprises and a shortage of consumer goods. State planning was never flexible enough to cope with the complexities of a post-war economy.

Unofficial arrangements between manufacturers to overcome the shortcomings of the planning system were essential. The economy would not have functioned without. As might be predicted, this practice of circumventing the plan became widespread, despite the severe punishment occasionally meted out to those whose indiscretions proved a challenge to the fundamentals of communism. At the same time a black market for consumer goods flourished.

The Stasi were aware of the black market but seldom moved to prevent it. Allowing innocent citizens to acquire life's little luxuries by illicit trading made them vulnerable to coercion. A Stasi officer would summon an individual to a local HQ and with a stern face inform him or her that they had been under observation. The hapless individual would then be confronted with the evidence of black market dealings. This amounted to economic crime for which the punishment was "Umerziehung" to correct corrupt capitalist tendencies. A few days after this preliminary encounter another, more avuncular Stasi officer would visit the home of the targeted person and express sympathy for his or her plight. Then, with a promise to spare the individual the disgrace of arrest, *de-qualification* and the need to take employment as a menial, the Stasi officer would coerce him or her into serving as an informer or undertaking certain distasteful missions. There being no possibility of employment other than in state run enterprises the hapless individual had no choice but to comply.

In some instances totally innocent and inoffensive people found themselves inveigled into wholly illicit activities masterminded by corrupt members of the *Partei* in positions of authority in the government.

Merchant seamen with their access to foreign ports were particularly prone to this sort of exploitation. A typical case was that of a Schiffsbetrieb deck officer who had been blackmailed into a smuggling racket of a truly unusual nature: fake antiques.

In the year 1710, financed by the King of Poland and Elector of Saxony, Johann Friedrich Bottger, a potter who specialised in cobalt blue and onion pattern porcelain, opened a factory in Meissen, near Dresden, an East German city. Throughout the eighteenth and nineteenth centuries and on into the present era, Meissen enjoyed worldwide renown for the excellence of its porcelain. According to the rumours circulating, the good name attached to this heritage industry was being exploited for illicit purposes. A clandestine workshop was producing fake Meissen chinaware and arranging for it to be sold as genuine antiques to eager collectors around the world. The proceeds from this business were deposited in a numbered bank account in a Caribbean tax haven. Given that East German citizens were permitted to receive presents from abroad, it is very likely that this money was used to pay for the import of luxury goods from capitalist countries. The Schiffsbetrieb officer had been very reluctant to get involved but the promise that his teenage son would not be prosecuted for some minor misdemeanour was sufficient to persuade him. The East German government official who masterminded this trade and coerced the innocent seaman into this smuggling racket was never identified.

So it was with chief engineer Otto Hengerer, whose nephew had been accused of some unspecified and remote involvement in the tunnel that had been dug from a derelict house in East Berlin under the Wall and on into West Berlin. He came under scrutiny because his TV aerial pointed towards West Berlin and this was considered an indication of his interest in West German TV programmes and western propaganda directed at undermining the Democratic Republic of East Germany.

A deputy minister in the Ausenhandelsministerium discovered that Otto's nephew was under observation and summoned Otto to the Ministry. With veiled threats mixed with bonhomie, the ship's engineer was drawn into a scheme which involved the smuggling of titanium and other metals of value out of the DDR for sale in capitalist countries. The metals in question were to be delivered to Otto's ship in the form of spare parts for the engine. All Otto had to do was to arrange for them to be off-loaded by ship's crane on to the quay into waiting transport in whatever port he was told to off-load them. It was all so simple and innocuous, except that Otto knew that the spares thus delivered could never be used to service the marine engines he was responsible for. His complicity was essential for the scheme to operate smoothly; he had to account for the higher than average use of spares.

Captain Mueller, like so many others, found himself ensnared by the Stasi entirely due to misfortune. His brother-in-law had given him a West German magazine to read in which there was an article about chess. As fate decreed in that same magazine there was also an article which was considered detrimental to the East German government. The article concerned "die Rache des Papstes",

In October 1969 a telecommunications tower erected by the East German government was ceremoniously inaugurated. Located in Alexander Platz, East Berlin and with an overall height of 368 metres, it loomed threateningly over West Berlin. It was a symbol of East German power reminding the citizens of West Berlin that the "Wall" was only a short bike ride away. In 1970 as early spring turned to late spring, the sun rose higher and higher in the sky and in the afternoons, when it was in the West, its rays were reflected by the glazing in the dome at the top of the tower. This reflection of the sun took the form of a fiery crucifix, a symbol of Christianity, a religion which communism sought to eradicate. In the press of the free world the irony of the situation proved a source of merriment that had to be exploited. It was a story that just ran and ran: the East Germans, albeit unwittingly, displaying a crucifix on their most prestigious structure. It was something they nobody could have imagined, not even in a wildest dream. But, for the people of West Berlin it was a moral booster; they called it "die Rache des Papstes", the Pope's revenge. The East German authorities tried everything they could to prevent the sun reflecting a fiery crucifix but all their attempts failed. In the end they announced to the world that it was not a cross but a plus sign indicating that life in the East was a *"plus"*.

A malevolent junior officer serving with Mueller and whom Mueller had had occasion to reprimand for incompetence, reported to the Schiffsbetrieb that the captain had been seen reading a magazine in which there was a reference to "die Rache des Papstes". During an interrogation Mueller claimed that he had found the magazine somewhere but could not recall where. He had no intention of revealing that it was his brother-in-law who had given it to him. The shipping company administration accepted that he had just casually picked the magazine up and assured him that the matter was closed. Nonetheless, he knew that he had been compromised and that if he didn't want the investigation to go further and involve his brother-in-law, at some future time he might feel compelled to undertake something illicit.

On no less than three separate occasions, a shore-based senior captain had summoned Mueller to his office and had given him a pocket-sized packet with instructions to deliver it to a private address in a port of call that his ship was to put into. He was warned not to enquire what was in the packet and to keep it locked in the safe in his cabin whilst at sea. Although he would have preferred to refuse, Mueller complied on all three occasions; he was aware of the unspoken but very evident threat that if he were to refuse the Stasi might be tipped off and there would be an enquiry into where the magazine had come from. Nevertheless, it was repugnant to him. Being coerced into making clandestine deliveries in foreign ports and maybe risking smuggling charges, was not at all the way in which he had hoped his career would develop when first serving as a cadet. For all that, he was better placed than chief engineer Otto. He could deny ever having been sent on such missions, whereas Otto needed to falsify his engine room repair log book in order to account for the fake spare parts.

During these three missions to deliver the packets whose contents were a mystery to him, he always came away with the impression that the clandestine recipients of the packets took possession of them with an undue nonchalance. On the fourth mission, when the ship was in Pernambucco, doing as instructed he went ashore to find the contact who, like the three other previous contacts, treated the packet with a thinly disguised indifference. However, this time was different; he was given a packet to take back with him. There had been vague talk about not only delivering but also bringing packets back to the base on the Baltic and leaving them in the safe in his captain's cabin for later collection by unspecified persons. Mueller took the packet hesitatingly, all the while trying to think of an excuse for not taking it. He was deep in the mire; on this occasion they expected him to smuggle something into his country. This by itself was sufficient to cause him anxiety. In addition to this, he detected something in his contact's demeanour which left him uneasy. It contrasted with the nonchalance with which the man had received the packet he had just delivered.

On the way back to the Rosa Luxemburg, he was deep in thought. It was clear to him that the first three packets he had delivered were dummies which most likely contained nothing more than newspaper. The purpose of these previous missions was to test him so as to be sure that he was capable of delivering a packet, unopened and without asking questions. As he walked through the busy Pernambucco streets he could not stop thinking about what had occurred and try as he might he was forced to conclude that the packet he had just been given probably contained something which anywhere in the world would be considered contraband. His misgivings intensified when, as he arrived at the dock gates, he noticed a man whom he had spotted lurking outside the house where he had met the contact. On previous missions to deliver packets he was not aware of being shadowed. It was then that he began to wonder whether he should try to re-board his ship with the packet in his pocket or perhaps dump it somewhere. It was not certain that he would be able to dispose of it without being seen by the man tailing him. If he were caught with it in his possession, local customs officers would be entitled to enquire what it contained. Claiming total ignorance of its contents would make him look suspicious, not to say foolish.

As it happened, all around the world, ships from communist countries were noted for their strict discipline and customs officers in many ports were of the opinion that seamen from these ships were unlikely to be carrying contraband and so in many instances they were content to carry out only token inspections.

Captain Mueller strode through the dock gates unhindered. As soon as regained the privacy of his cabin, he locked the packet in the safe and began to breathe more easily. Nonetheless, he knew he was trapped and in every free moment, when not preoccupied with his duties, his mind returned to the question of how to recover his unsullied status as a professional seaman.

NINE

In 1971, East Germany became a member of the United Nations and in 1973 many countries exchanged ambassadors with East Germany, amongst them the UK and France. Only a short time elapsed before these newly forged relations were put to the test by a fire which broke out on an East German cargo vessel in the middle of the English Channel. The situation was dire and the captain sent an SOS to the French authorities.

Less than twelve hours after sending the SOS, the blazing vessel had crossed the Channel and was lying at anchor in Poole Bay, just to the south of Boscombe Pier. When the residents of Bournemouth East Cliff awoke that sunny, summer day and saw a ship with clouds of smoke enveloping its superstructure, what they were seeing was the Rosa Luxemburg.

The Dorsetshire Fire Brigade was summoned and took charge of the situation. By the time the fire had been extinguished most of the curious public had dispersed. Only the guests in the first class hotels and the residents in the luxury mansion remained to keep the vessel under observation. Those who had binoculars and who were familiar with the International Code of Signals, knew the significance of the flags flying from the ship's mast. The yellow "Q" flag indicated to the customs authorities that the ship had arrived "from foreign" whilst the UK commercial fleet ensign, known as the "red duster" showed respect for tradition and courtesy observed by seafarers when in another country's waters. The ensign fluttering over the stern may not have been widely recognised as East German.

An HM customs launch, recognisable by its blue ensign, still lay alongside the stricken cargo ship and on deck there was much activity. It was evident that the authorities were involved in something more complex than customs clearance and a fire on board a foreign registered ship.

Earlier that morning, when the sun was just visible behind Hurst Castle, the captain ordered the remaining lifeboat to be lowered into the water. He and the chief engineer together with two deck hands who had not been evacuated by the French rescue services went ashore. Only the third officer, three ordinary seamen, two engine room mechanics and the radio operator stayed on board as watchmen. Later they were joined by the two deck hands who had put the two senior officers ashore and then brought the lifeboat back to the ship.

Boscombe Pier had no landing stage that they could see and so they came ashore on Bournemouth Pier, clambering over the turnstiles to get to the promenade. Otto, who spoke quite passable English, stopped a man walking his dog and asked the way to the nearest police station.

In the police station in Landsdowne, they sat drinking tea awaiting the arrival of immigration officers who were to assess their claims for political asylum.

Meanwhile in France, the ship's crew evacuated by

the SNSM had been landed in Cherbourg. The sick crew members were being cared for and the others were being interviewed by the French authorities. The Quai d'Orsay, the French foreign office, proved quite co-operative when East German diplomatic staff requested permission to go to Cherbourg to provide the evacuated sailors with consular assistance. Apart from these consular duties, the diplomats in France had another, more important objective. They needed to investigate the circumstances of the emergency which had caused the crew abandon ship. To preserve the good name of the DDR (East Germany), it was vital to establish the facts and report on them before the world's press could have a chance to publish an alternative more sensational version. Two crew members were particularly forthcoming and provided very detailed accounts of what had occurred.

Boatswain Wolfgang Kunnel's seagoing career began as a teenager in the 1930s, during the early years of the Third Reich and before the outbreak of the second world war. Even as a member of the Hitler Jugend, he was not at ease with Nazism and after the war he quickly gravitated to Marxism-Leninism. Now nearly fifty, he was an experienced seaman, a dedicated communist and a Stasi informer.

Political officer Hermann Schneider was barely five years old when the war ended. His father had been lost at sea in 1942 and his mother had been killed during the last days of the war. The director of the orphanage where he was brought up was a staunch member of the *"Partei"* and the only father he knew. Schneider was a committed communist, a loyal *"Partei"* member and a Stasi officer.

What boatswain Kunnel and political officer Schneider

told their embassy officials was quite startling. There was much to tell. The hatch covers open to the weather, the second officer presumed lost overboard and the fire in number four hold. In return, what the embassy officials told them was equally startling: the Rosa Luxemburg was lying at anchor in Poole Bay some sixty nautical miles away on the other side of the English Channel.

The news about the Rosa Luxemburg had come from diplomats in the East German Embassy in London. They, as representatives of the owners of the vessel, had been contacted by the UK authorities and courteously reminded of their obligations under UK merchant shipping legislation. The recently appointed diplomatic staff suddenly found themselves confronted with a crisis which they had not envisaged and for which they were not prepared. There was a frenetic exchange of encoded messages between the embassy staff and the DDR foreign ministry, the Schiffsbetrieb and the Kriegsmarine. As it happened the UK and East Germany had not yet exchanged naval attaches and so among the embassy staff there was no experienced seafarer to assume control of the investigation into what had occurred. The Schiffsbetrieb wanted an immediate report on the state of the vessel, its seaworthiness, the state of the cargo and whether the confidential books had been jettisoned or whether they were still on board. Nobody at the embassy had the training or the experience to provide answers to such important, technical questions. The DDR made a formal approach to the Soviet Union for expert assistance and it was agreed that the Soviet naval attache in London would be entrusted with the task. Accordingly, Victor Ivanovitch Krutinsky applied for permission to go to Bournemouth on behalf of the DDR whilst arrangements could be made with the Foreign Office for an East German naval officer to be given provisional accreditation and sent the UK specifically to take charge of the matter.

TEN

It was near midday when the Lotus Flower with Oscar on board approached the estuary of the River Dart. The day mark on top of the cliff was clearly visible and at sea level the outline of the Mew Stone could just be distinguished against the rocky shore.

This was the moment to raise the yellow "Q" flag signifying to HM Customs that the vessel had just come from "foreign" and that the crew were "healthy". Once inside the estuary with Dartmouth Castle abeam, the skipper told his crew to look out for a vacant mooring buoy, preferably somewhere on the Kingswear side of the river. Given that there was an extra person on board, one who had not been declared as a crew member on departure and who was not a UK citizen, the correct procedure was to pick up a buoy and wait for customs officers to board the vessel.

A vacant buoy was spotted and for brief instant the skipper wondered whether, as a concluding sail training exercise, he would have the crew pick it up under sail. However, there was too much traffic for a novice crew to carry out such a manoeuvre and so he started the engine and ordered the sails to be lowered. Once securely moored to a buoy it was time to go below have a cup of tea or instant coffee and wait for custom officers to board.

Some ten minutes later the sounds of an engine and voices, then feet on the upper deck heralded the arrival of the customs officers.

"Did you have a good trip?" came a voice followed by a man in navy blue uniform descending from the cockpit into the saloon. He surveyed the assembled crew, all seated and enjoying a "cuppa".

"Does anybody have anything to declare?"

It was the skipper who answered.

"Yes. Apart from a few bottles of booze, for which each of us must be individually accountable, we have to declare that we have one extra passenger. We found him on a raft floating in the sea a mile or so north of Alderney. He says his name is Oscar. He speaks some English. We've not asked him for his papers so we know nothing about him, except that he's a shipwrecked sailor."

The customs officer took on a concerned look. He had expected that the arrival of the Lotus Flower would be no more than routine: fill in a few forms, get some signatures and return to other duties. A shipwrecked sailor was likely to involve him in a mass of paperwork.

Later that afternoon, Oscar was taken to Exeter to be medically examined and then interviewed by immigration officials. Although he could speak some English, it was thought preferable and fairer to him not to start the screening procedure without an interpreter. It took time to find a competent, accredited German speaking interpreter and so for this and other reasons, the interview did not begin until the following morning.

The first interview was devoted to establishing his identity, date of birth, place of birth, marital status, parents names and dates and places of birth. Then he was asked about his schooling and professional training and qualifications.

In the afternoon a second interview took place during which he was invited to explain how he came to be adrift on a raft in the English Channel.

Oscar was manifestly pleased to find himself face to face with an immigration officer asking him to tell his story. He was greatly encouraged by the courteous attitude of all the officials he met since the moment he had been taken ashore in Dartmouth. He felt sure that they had no intention of sending him back to East Germany against his will. He was further reassured by the meticulous manner in which everything he said was written down. Surely, taking such trouble to interview him must indicate that his case would be considered seriously. He sat forward in his chair, desperately keen to be seen to co-operate. Nonetheless, he felt tired, albeit pleasantly tired.

He explained how he had been unnerved by the length of Schneider' triple encoded radio message sent to company HQ. He felt sure that it was about him and that his correspondence with Erica had been discovered. Once back in their home port he would have a lot of explaining to do. His misgivings were further intensified by the way in which Schneider had taken to looking at him, even staring at him, especially in the officers' quarters.

A plan of escape from the ship and East Germany which he had toyed with many times in the past, came back and exercised his mind. When not fully occupied with his duties he could think of nothing else. He would "jump ship" in the

Dover Straits and attempt to reach the shores of France by swimming or paddling some floating object that he would throw overboard. The more he thought through the final details of the plan, the more he dismissed it as a wholly impractical proposition; his chances of reaching any beach in the Pas de Calais were nil. Moreover, if he were seen "jumping ship" and were then "rescued" by his shipmates, his career as an officer in East Germany's merchant marine would be ended. Years of hard labour would be all that he could expect and no chance of seeing Erica again.

Nonetheless, he was in a "now or never" mood and his determination to escape and join Erica dominated all his thoughts. When on the bridge reading the meteorological reports, he saw that the ship would encounter a storm in the approach to the English Channel and that this would be followed by fog. Slowly but surely a plan took shape. At night and in fog somewhere off the French coast he could launch one of the old wooden rafts that lay about on the midship deck and slip overboard on to it without being noticed. Aboard a raft, rather than immersed in water, there would be less risk of hypothermia. He would only have to survive till sunrise and then hope to be picked up by a passing vessel, trusting that it was not a communist flagged one.

The immigration officer paused, put down his pen, leant back in his chair and said with a genuinely warm smile :

"Well! I would never have imagined anybody taking such a risk. That was a really bold decision, casting yourself adrift like that. Few people would have the courage to do it."

Oscar appeared confused by this expression of admiration. He felt that it was a disguised challenge to the veracity of his story and so he continued his narrative persuaded that the more details he provided the more he would be believed.

He explained that during the storm, with the engine room flooded and all hands engaged in saving the ship, he knew that a better chance to "jump ship" would never come again. Added to which, he could not evade the stark truth: it was he who had supervised the closing of the hatches. Although sure at the time that all had been secured in accordance with the procedure set out in the manual, seeing the cascades of water pouring into the hold he began to have doubts about his competence. Had he been nonchalant in the performance of his duties or perhaps too distracted with thoughts of Erica, he asked himself. Excluding professional negligence, the only other explanation was that somebody had tampered with hatch covers. This meant that there was a saboteur on board. Come what may, he would be blamed and this could only worsen his position once back in their home port. Seeing the boatswain and the whole crew fully occupied in closing the hatches and feeling sure that the ship was not about to sink, he saw his chance and on the spur of the moment hid in the chain locker. With the ship pitching and rolling and huge waves landing on the deck, nobody would be aware of his disappearance. Indeed, subsequent events proved him right.

He went on to say that in the chain locker he was careful to ensure that he had good ventilation and so stayed close to the hatch which he propped open with some slivers of wood. Ferrous objects like anchor chains, in the process of rusting, can deplete the oxygen concentration in an enclosed space and anybody spending time in a chain locker risks death by asphyxiation.

Firmly decided not to conceal any detail, Oscar spoke freely. He wanted to win the trust of the UK immigration service and so was at great pains to hold nothing back. His own good sense told him that only by being totally truthful could he validate and indeed expedite his application for asylum in West Germany. Rejoining Erica in Hamburg and starting a new life was his sole objective.

Erica, was the daughter of Volga Germans who at the end of the Second World War had abandoned their homes in Russia to resettle back in the land of their ancestors. They were the descendants of an eastward migration of Germans to the Volga region in the eighteenth century. Catherine the Great, who was herself German born, instigated this migration because at that time the lands around the Volga were sparsely populated. Catherine thought that the best way to prevent the Turks from seizing this fringe Russian territory, was to occupy and develop it. Accordingly she encouraged farming folk from Germany to migrate to the Volga. There they lived quietly for six generations, as German people, speaking German and observing German traditions. Hitler's incursion into Russia as far as the Volga in 1942 aroused much antagonism on the part of the Russians toward this ethnic enclave and after the war many of these Volga Germans chose to depart in search of a new life in Germany.

Sotchi, a Soviet holiday resort on the Black Sea, was a place where many Russians would go on summer vacation to be restored to health in the local sanatoria. It was also a destination for adventurous tourists from Western European countries. They wanted a holiday with a difference, in a country that few would think of visiting and the Soviet authorities were glad to have the hard currency that these holidaymakers brought with them.

Apart from this, it was a place where East met West. Families separated by the Iron Curtain and the Berlin Wall seized the opportunity to meet long lost relatives on the beaches in Sotchi. Erica went to Sotchi every year for three years in the hope of finding some trace of her cousins who had remained in the Volga Region. She met Schulz instead. She literally bumped into him on the street outside Hotel Magnolia where she was staying.

Their paths were about to cross and so they both stepped aside to avoid each other. As it happened despite these manoeuvres, they collided. Faltering attempts to apologise in Russian revealed that neither of them had a full command of that language. Switching to English did not facilitate communication. It was then that they discovered that they both spoke German.

They exchanged personal details as people do when on holiday: names, nationality and how long they were going to stay in Sotchi. They might then have both gone on their way if Oscar had not noticed that Erica was wearing a brooch with three horizontal stripes, yellow over blue over yellow.

"How curious! In the International Code of Signals your brooch is exactly the same as the flag meaning : *Keep clear of me - I am manoeuvring with difficulty.*"

She laughed and said :

"Are you are sailor?"

"Yes."

Then with unaccustomed boldness he added :

"I'm tired. Shall we sit down for a moment?"

They spent more than an hour together and parted only after having agreed to meet again the next day.

If either of them had been asked if they believed in love at first sight, both would have scoffed at the idea: that sort of thing only happens in fairy tales. But, this is what did happen. When the time came for them to part they were firmly determined to meet again and had devised a plan by which they might write to each other without anybody becoming aware of their correspondence.

ELEVEN

Oscar Schulz was feeling more and more relaxed as his debriefing progressed; he would soon be on his way to Hamburg to join Erica. What a surprise she would get. He had asked for pen and paper to write her a letter and planned to telephone her as soon as could. As he sat talking to immigration officers explaining that he wanted asylum in West Germany, he was totally unaware of what had happened on the Rosa Luxemburg after he had made his escape. It was no part of an immigration officer's duty to reveal such confidential details. He did not know that the ship was lying at anchor in Poole Bay and that the captain and the chief engineer had also asked for asylum. They too were being interviewed by immigration officers, not in Exeter, but in Southampton.

The same procedure applied. They were both asked for their bio-data and then individually invited to tell their story. Chief engineer Otto Hengerer explained how he had been coerced into criminality, false accounting and smuggling. He told his story from the point of view of man who was proud of his profession. He was a ship's engineer and resented being exploited and even exposed to imprisonment in a foreign country, all for the benefit of a corrupt superior.

In the case of captain Fritz Mueller, the same procedure was followed, with one essential difference. His asylum application did not divest him of his responsibilities for the Rosa Luxemburg. As captain he was still liable under UK merchant shipping legislation for its seaworthiness and safe conduct whilst in UK territorial waters. He insisted that he had not wilfully or wittingly infringed any merchant shipping regulation and that his ship, now at anchor, had endangered neither person nor property in UK coastal waters. By asking for asylum he had surrendered his command, but not irresponsibly. He had left the ship in the hands of the third officer, a competent seaman.

These matters aside, he was still required to give a full report on all that had taken place aboard: the missing hatch covers, the fire and not least the loss overboard of the second officer. In this respect, the immigration officers interviewing him held an ace card; they knew the truth about second officer Schulz's apparent loss overboard. The explanation he gave tallied with the story that Schulz had told, so adding to his credibility. Unlike some other asylum seekers, he was turning out to be genuine and reliable.

Captain Mueller, without understanding the reasons why, detected that his interrogators believed what he was telling them. Their body language showed that they had begun to trust him. The moment had come to tell the full story and reveal all the details of the packages he had been coerced into delivering; especially the one given to him in Pernambuco. He was at great pains to insist that he had no idea what it contained but suspected that it was something prohibited. He gave them the key to the safe in his cabin and was reassured to see that the response to this item of intelligence was immediate. As soon as the key could be delivered to Bournemouth, customs officers went aboard, opened the safe and retrieved the package. It contained cocaine.

Captain Mueller, when he was told that the package contained a narcotic, said that it was evidently for the personal use of somebody in the Schiffsbetrieb but had no inkling who that person might be. His instructions were to lock the package in the safe and leave it there to be collected by persons unknown on his return to the home port. This firm evidence was an unequivocal confirmation of his bona fides. He relaxed in his chair; without doubt, his unwillingness to be drawn into drug smuggling would serve to prove that if granted asylum he would be a law abiding citizen.

TWELVE

The Rosa Luxemburg was a knotty problem requiring a solution. In the upper echelons of government there was a clear will to avoid any administrative decision which might sour the recently established relations with East Germany. At the same time the maritime authorities felt compelled to enforce merchant shipping legislation concerning the seaworthiness and conduct of vessels in UK waters. Safety required that no indulgence be shown. Urgent meetings took place between the various responsible authorities and there were many telephone calls to the East German Embassy. Painstakingly, the divers parties reached a unanimous conclusion. The interests of all concerned would be best served if the Rosa Luxemburg were to get underway, leave UK waters and make passage to her home port. In order to facilitate this, all administrative hindrances preventing the ship from weighing anchor must be overcome.

A report on the seaworthiness of the ship carried out by DTI inspectors stated that the Rosa Luxemburg was in a fit state to put to sea. The vessel's hull and machinery remained undamaged. Although the cause of the fire had not yet been determined, it had been fully extinguished and there was no danger that it would flare up again. At the same time, but independently of the DTI, the third officer drafted a report for the Schiffsbetrieb and had it endorsed by the Soviet Naval Attache. It confirmed the DTI inspectors' conclusion that the ship was seaworthy. However, other problems remained.

The fact that both the captain and chief engineer had asked for asylum meant that the ship would have to reach its home port without its two most senior officers. Moreover, the crew remaining on board would not be sufficient to man the ship during a passage lasting several days. There was an obvious solution: arrange for the crew evacuated by the French SNSM, to be brought from Cherbourg to Southampton. However, this would involve visas for all and other considerable paperwork both in France and in the UK. In contrast, there would be fewer visas and associated formalities if certain key crew members in France could be flown to Hurn Airport and then brought by road to Bournemouth. Moreover, it would be quicker and cheaper. The East German Handelsmarine agreed to this plan.

Four of the crew were selected to be flown across the Channel. Amongst them was the first officer who, thanks to the treatment received in a French hospital, was almost fully recovered from the enteritis which had confined him to the sick bay. He would be appointed acting captain. Joining him would be the political officer who was also a competent watch keeper, the boatswain and a junior engineer officer.

The plan was for the Rosa Luxemburg to enter the Grand Rade at Cherbourg where the crew would be waiting in the ship's lifeboats ready to climb aboard. After the lifeboats had been hoisted back on deck, the vessel would be able to get underway and make passage back to her home port.

Nevertheless, a complex administrative entanglement needed to be unravelled. It was essential to placate all parties, dedicated as they were to the conscientious fulfilment of the duties entrusted to them. There were the sticklers for compliance with the rule book and respect for procedure. They maintained that a master of a foreign registered ship should not imagine that he could enter British waters, drop the hook and scurry ashore to claim asylum, abandoning his ship to the command of a junior officer. Others were more flexible. For them, all that was necessary was to allay their fears that at a subsequent date they might be subject to disciplinary measures for allowing the ship to get underway before all formalities had been completed. The obstacles seemed insuperable until a compromise solution emerged. All parties undertook not to challenge a proposal that came from the very highest level of government. In accordance with this proposal, they were all to acknowledge that the ship would be in danger of grounding on Bournemouth's sandy beaches in the southerly gale that was forecast for the end of the week. Without doubt, a ship aground on the beach of a popular holiday resort would be a costly disaster and blame would attach to them for not having taken all necessary measures to prevent such a catastrophe. Therefore, it was agreed that as soon as there was sufficient crew aboard, the ship should get underway and not be impeded by bureaucracy.

THIRTEEN

The political officer had been very active during the crew's brief stay in Cherbourg. Once he had recovered from smoke inhalation, he took stock of the situation. In the absence of the captain and the chief engineer, whom he had always suspected were not true communists, he had to step into the breach and assume command. It was the principal duty of a political officer on board a cargo ship to keep the crew together in accordance with good Marxist-Leninist doctrine. There would be a thorough enquiry once the ship docked in their home port and although in no way to blame for any of the mishaps that had occurred, the fact that they had occurred whilst he was on board would reflect badly on his record. He might redeem himself if he were able to rally the crew and to raise their morale.

Schneider assembled his fellow shipmates and spoke to them in an unusually informal and friendly manner. His tone of voice and smiling face contrasted starkly with the surly and unapproachable *Partei* member they had come to know aboard ship. It was a traditional communist pep talk, full of well rehearsed rhetoric. He assured them that their ship was seaworthy and that they should continue to serve without fear. He explained that all the unfortunate accidents had been due to sabotage on the part of those traitors to their Fatherland who had abandoned them to their fate in order to claim asylum in the UK. He rounded off his speech with a broad smile and reassuring words.

"We are now homeward bound to Rostock" he said, as he and the boatswain shook hands.

Only one recalcitrant deckhand was not persuaded by Schneider. Later that day he asked the French authorities for asylum. He was not married and so had no concerns about what would happen to his family back in East Germany.

As the Rosa Luxemburg cleared the Fort de L'Ouest and set a course for the Straits of Dover, Schneider began to review the events of the past few days. He would be expected to make a lengthy report and answer a barrage of questions. Crucially, before docking he would need to decide who was responsible for the sabotage. Because they had defected, the captain and the chief engineer were an obvious choice upon whom to lay the blame. Without doubt, they were criminals and enemies of the East German State who had not thought twice about endangering the ship and her crew in order to arrange their defection. In his 2500 word triple-encoded despatch to the Schiffsbetrieb, he had made known his suspicions about Otto Hengerer's involvement in the smuggling of spare parts and false accounting in the engine room's documentation. He told himself that it would be an easy matter to persuade his superiors that Mueller and Hengerer were not only smugglers but also saboteurs.

Nonetheless, deep within his inner being he knew he had no conclusive proof of these allegations and that the real culprit might still be on board, undetected and ready to commit sabotage again. The more he thought about it the more unlikely it seemed that two tried and trusted seamen like Mueller and Hengerer would resort to reckless endangerment of the ship merely to facilitate their defection. It did not surprise him that they should have betrayed their country and asked for asylum in a capitalist country; he knew them to be lukewarm in their attitude to the *Partei*. However, removing hatch covers and setting fire to the cargo was something that no professional seaman would ever do. For this reason, despite repeated demands from Schiffsbetrieb, he hesitated to send a fuller interim report and so avoided naming Mueller and Hengerer as the guilty parties. What if there were a further act of sabotage, he asked himself. He would be shown to be wrong and would appear foolish in front of his superiors. This thought plagued his mind, especially when on watch and solely responsible for the conduct of the ship. However, there were brief moments when another thought impressed itself upon him. Perhaps a more likely culprit was the young deckhand who had decided to claim asylum in France. Werner Schwarz was a meek young man whose mild manner rendered almost invisible. In the Stasi training school, they had been made aware that sometimes spies and saboteurs are at pains to make themselves inconspicuous.

Schneider was in a quandary. There were more questions than answers. If the deckhand was the saboteur, what of Mueller and Hengerer? Did they simply seize the opportunity afforded them by the fire to arrange their defection? Was it credible that they could have so speedily and secretly agreed between themselves to take the blazing ship across the Channel to anchor in UK waters? It was a clever plan: leave him, the political officer stranded in France whilst they claimed asylum in another jurisdiction and in so doing, put themselves wholly beyond his reach.

He was still debating who to blame in his report when the Rosa Luxemburg was off Cap Gris Nez in the Dover Separation Zone. It was at this point that a plain text signal from Shiffsbetrieb in Rostock addressed to the whole of the East German merchant fleet resolved the dilemma. The Handelsmarine Minister had informed the government that captain Fritz Mueller and chief engineer Otto Hengerer were solely to blame for the endangerment of the Rosa Luxemburg.

How to draft his report had suddenly become clear. Nobody in the Schiffsbetrieb would dare to argue with the minister.

⚭⚭⚭

A gale force southerly wind blew salty spume on to the under cliff road all along the Bournemouth sea front. Huge waves crashed onto the promenade leaving behind masses of sand as the water drained back on to the beach. High above on the Overcliff Drive, the hotel guests and residents of the luxury properties stared out onto a stormy sea. Across Poole Bay, between Anvil Point and the Needles, the waves were unusually high for the time of year. There was a chill in the air and the wind whistled around their balconies. As they looked, they became aware that the ship which had lain at anchor in the bay was no longer there. For a moment or two some of them were curious to know where it had gone to and why it had anchored in the bay in the first place. No explanation was to be found in mass media outlets; the story of the blazing ship had ceased to be front page news and the defection to the West of three of its officers had not yet been leaked to the press.

Days after the Rosa Luxemburg had left the bay experts from the Dorsetshire Fire Brigade published the results of their investigation into the causes of the fire. According to their findings it was due to the cargo of leaf tobacco being incorrectly dried and stowed. This, in the wrong conditions can lead to fermentation and fermentation generates heat. If the temperature rises above 50 degrees centigrade, spontaneous ignition is almost inevitable. No external heat source is necessary.

In the East German Handelsmarine, Mueller and Hengerer were denounced as defectors, traitors, smugglers and saboteurs. Long articles were written condemning them in the Schiffsbetrieb's newsletter. Schulz was almost forgotten, save by his friends. They remember him as a shipmate who lost his life in the service of the Fatherland.

The full story of what happened on board the Rosa Luxemburg when passage making from Cuba to Rostock has many more strands to it than the official reports may lead us to suppose.

Footnote:

Rosa Luxemburg 1871 - 1919 was a Polish-German revolutionary and a communist martyr, idolised in the German Democratic Republic.

FLIGHT FROM TIBET

A fictional account of events which
took place in March 1959

ONE

Bod is what the Tibetans call their country. Located in the Himalayas, between India and China, at heights above sea level from 10 000 feet in the south to 15 000 feet in the north, it is the Roof of the World. Mount Everest straddles its border with Nepal and rivers such as the Yangtze, the Yellow River, the Mekong, the Indus and the Ganges rise on its mountain plateau.

The Portuguese are said to be the first Europeans to have sent missionaries to Tibet. They were followed by others, including some British. Be that as it may, Tibet purged its territory of foreigners in the second quarter of the 19th century and shut its borders until 1904 when a Treaty was signed which allowed for a British Trade Agency to be established in the capital, Lhasa.

In 1927, John and Margaret Boyd, with their son Jeremy, aged three, were travelling in the Himalayas. During a visit to friends at the British Trade Agency they both fell ill and died. The orphaned Jeremy was entrusted to a Tibetan nanny by the staff of the agency until such times as arrangements could be made for him to be repatriated into the care of his kith and kin in Britain.

Jeremy's stay in Lhasa lasted longer than anyone would

have wished. Communications with the home country were slow and the process of finding relations willing to adopt the child involved lengthy enquiries. The net result was that the boy spent the early part of his childhood in the care of a Tibetan nanny and so acquired a native knowledge of the local idiom. When he finally returned home to Britain at the age of six, he spoke both English and a dialect of Tibetan, a difficult language for adult students to master.

Now a freelance journalist, aged thirty five, he found himself in India. The year was 1959 and the month March. There was turmoil in Tibet, the country where a local nanny had nursed him as a small boy and with whose children he had played until his departure in 1930 for boarding school in Britain.

The People's Republic of China, which had claimed Tibet as part of its national territory in 1951, was in the final stages of crushing a revolt that had broken out in 1956. The communisation of Tibet was in its early stages or as the new Chinese masters would have preferred to say, the "modernisation" of a backward province had just begun.

There were reports that thousands of Tibetans had perished in the insurrection and that Tibet's spiritual leader, the Dalai-lama, fearing capture by the Chinese was attempting to flee his homeland.

After much soul searching Jeremy decided that he was not indifferent to their plight; some of his earliest and fondest memories were of Lhasa and the nanny who had been so kind to him. He had not wholly forgotten the Tibetan he had learned from his substitute mother and the children who had been his companions in Lhasa. He found that listening to the stories told by Tibetan refugees recently arrived in

Nepal and India was not merely a saddening experience; it was also bewildering. He understood much of what they were saying whilst being almost incapable of repeating a single word. It was like a journey of discovery back into a strange land which paradoxically seemed familiar. Perhaps it was this inexplicable familiarity with an alien culture and a chance to relive forgotten moments in his childhood that persuaded him to go to Tibet and witness first hand the events which were becoming front page news. For him, a freelance journalist of independent means, a trip to Tibet would prove an opportunity to develop his career and also visit the place where his parents had died.

Having made his decision, all that remained was to find a way to enter Tibet without being stopped by the Chinese authorities. This was to take more time to arrange than he would have wanted.

<hr />

Potola Palace dominates Lhasa, the Tibetan capital. It is a large building 400 feet high and measuring 1300 by 1100 feet at its base. Built on a hill known as Marpo Ri, the Red Hill, it towers some 1000 feet above the valley, a principal geographical feature of the city. Consisting of 13 storeys and over 1000 rooms, a paranoiac despot wishing to foil assassination attempts could sleep in a different room each night for more than two and a half years before returning to the first room he slept in. Dating back to the 17th century, the Potala was the seat of government and the winter residence of the Dalai-lama, the spiritual and temporal leader of the Tibetan people.

Chinese General Ying in his headquarters looking out

onto the Potala was not sure whether the Dalai-lama was in the palace or at Norbulinka, his summer residence. The General wanted to arrest him discreetly in order not to arouse the antagonism of the Tibetan people, but the absence of precise intelligence on the whereabouts of the supreme spiritual leader thwarted him in this objective. Despite having thousands of well armed soldiers at his command in and around Lhasa, he was hesitant about storming the Potala. Such a display of force might prove a blunder. Built like a fortress, the palace was riddled with passages leading to a thousand rooms, all of which would be a perfect hiding place for his quarry. His masters in Peking were becoming impatient. The Dalai-lama was in breach of a minor clause in the 1951 treaty and so there was a perfect excuse to seize this Supreme Deity and with him control of the whole of Tibet. The delay in the execution of the plan was a source of exasperation in Chinese government circles. General Ying feared their displeasure.

Time and again since his arrival in the Tibetan capital he found himself recalling his days in Korea doing a real soldier's job: fighting the enemy. Defending his country's interests in war was what he had trained to do. Instead he found himself in command of an army whose mission was to strengthen communist China's grip on Tibet, minimize the influence of the Dalai-lama and win the hearts and minds of the Tibetan people. Despite his excellent war service, he knew that the price of failure would be the harsh regime of a labour camp working on the construction of dams and similar civil engineering projects. For a bowl of rice in the morning, another bowl at noon and in the evening no food, only a bowl of hot water, prisoners were expected to dig out two cubic meters of rock and soil per day or be denied any sort of nourishment. At his age it would be a prolonged death sentence. More than this servitude, he dreaded the disgrace attached to failure. He had devoted his entire life to the cause, to the revolution and to the People's Republic of China and felt that he had earned recognition and a pension, not the shame of a show trial, exclusion from all that was dear to him and death from exhaustion in a labour camp.

Tibet was not to his liking. It was a feudal theocracy in which mysticism abounded. He did not believe in the supernatural and had long since lost patience with the hoaxes his troops encountered almost daily. Amongst the lower ranks of the garrison in Lhasa there were rumours about Yetis kidnapping sentries in their sentry boxes during the night. He was sceptical about telepathy although some uncanny things had occurred which seemed to have been accomplished by thought transfer, if there were such a thing. He scoffed at the story he had been told about lamas seated out in the cold of mid-winter, raising their body temperature above 98.4 F by respiration alone and so melting the snow around them. Above all, his good sense refused to believe the myth that one lama could bring about the death of another by pure will power and that a duel had recently taken place in a dark room between two mystics each searching for the innermost soul of the other with the intent of extinguishing it.

On a practical front the lamas obstructed him in all his plans, displaying barely concealed hostility to Peking's attempts to modernise the country and bring its people the benefits of civilisation. The spiritual leaders of this mountainous, isolated land did not want to yield their power. They had for many long years resisted the use of the wheel and similar commonplace technology and were not about to welcome railways and airports.

If the Dalai-lama could be taken prisoner without ado, it might be possible to convince him that China was about to endow his country with great benefits. Isolated from his hootooktoos, the high priests of his entourage, this bespectacled twenty-four-year-old young man might succumb to a subtle blend of cajoling and veiled threats. The whole success of the mission depended on seizing this religious leader and persuading him to lend his support to the Chinese occupation and development plans. The general did not feel confident about the task entrusted to him; it was a job for a politician and he was a soldier.

The necessity for the mission, however, was evident. Apart from modernising Tibet and spreading communism, the government in Peking was pursuing objectives which were not wholly benevolent. Tibet's mineral wealth and geographical position were crucial. A country like China with 25% of the world's population and only 10% of the world's resources felt compelled to exploit its historical claim to what it had always considered to be a province. Moreover Tibet's strategic position as the source of numerous important rivers and a buffer between India and China weighed heavily in the balance.

General Ying fixed his gaze on the Potala, wondering how best to proceed.

༺✦༻

In the east of the country the Khambas were engaged in a losing battle with superior Chinese military forces.

Unlike the invading army, they had neither artillery nor air-cover. This latter disadvantage was offset by the fog which swathed the mountains, offering some concealment. It was strongly rumoured that the Khambas were supported by the CIA and had been receiving aid and training from that source since the 1956 uprising began. Nevertheless, without direct American intervention, especially from the US Air Force, these fearless guerrillas were no match for the better equipped and numerically superior Chinese regular army.

Aten, a PoTsoung (militia officer) mounted his horse and set off towards Lhasa carrying a message for the hootooktoos in the Potala. A skilled horseman and mountaineer he knew all the off-road tracks leading to the capital city and would have no difficulty eluding the Chinese army foot patrols. His mission was of vital importance to Tibet, his homeland. The message he carried must be delivered.

Six foot tall, Aten was essentially of nomad stock, born and raised in the rugged land of Cham. Tibetan by nationality, he spoke the nomad dialect in stentorian tones, a characteristic that distinguished him from the softer voiced population of Lhasa. Like all Khambas he was a practising Buddhist, dedicated to his country and the Dalai-lama. Travellers have told tales of Khambas so dedicated that they were prepared to sacrifice their lives on a single word of command from a superior. Others speak of them as robbers and bandits.

The Tibetan irregulars were outnumbered ten to one by the Chinese army but had three major advantages; their native of knowledge of the terrain, the mountain fog which hid them from Chinese spotter planes and their valour. How long could they resist the advance of the enemy contingents and what would the supreme spiritual leader decide to do in order to escape capture? These were the thoughts occupying Aten's mind as he rode westward.

The Chinese military commander in Lhasa had demanded that the Dalai-lama attend a meeting in army headquarters on 10th March and that he come alone without his retinue, which normally consisted of twenty five armed elite soldiers. The Tibetan people on learning of this development took to the streets to protest against what they considered to be an obvious attempt to abduct their Kundun and deport him to Peking.

No Khamba would betray His Holiness, Aten felt sure. The men he had left behind in their camp near the Tsangpo river were fiercely loyal and ready to fight to the last man. When pitted one-to-one against the enemy, they were invincible as was shown by their last skirmish in which they attacked a Chinese military convoy in a narrow gorge. After having destroyed five large lorries with grenades, they escaped into the mountains leaving a further ten lorries ablaze, all without any casualties on their side. The Chinese troops did not venture to pursue their attackers.

The Lhasa skyline was visible on the horizon and Aten started to give thought to how he might enter the city without being stopped by Chinese sentries in the cordon surrounding the capital. He reined his horse and turned towards a copse near some buildings lying outside the city precincts.

❦

In the Indian city of Tezpur, in the province of Assam, Jeremy Boyd after a long search had found a Tibetan guide willing to accompany him on his journey into Tibet. At first it seemed that he would never find a suitable man. Those whom he considered reliable and worthy were reluctant to offer their services to a European on a mission such as he proposed. They claimed it was too dangerous because the chances of being caught by the Chinese were great and the consequences for a Tibetan far worse than for a European. Regardless of how much money was being offered, they were not prepared to leave the relative security of their refugee status in India to shepherd a journalist over the mountains into Tibet and on to Lhasa.

Frustrated and desperate, Jeremy acquired a complete outfit of used Tibetan clothes and started to take conversation lessons from some refugee lamas in order to activate his passive knowledge of a language learned in childhood. It would be hazardous, even foolhardy, but if he could not find a guide, he would set off by himself and see how far he got. As a freelance journalist without an editor to please, he could do as he chose and might even accumulate sufficient material with which to write a book recounting his failed attempt to reach Lhasa.

It was during one of his conversation lessons that he was approached by Lozang, a young Tibetan of about thirty years. Lozang had noticed that Jeremy, dressed in Tibetan garb, did not appear excessively European. His features, burnished by the hot sun of India and crowned by Tibetan headgear, gave him a slightly Himalayan appearance. Moreover, he could converse in basic Tibetan, albeit somewhat falteringly but with much of the delivery and intonation of a native speaker. Reassured by Jeremy's newly emerged Tibetan alter ego, Lozang offered his services as a guide to Lhasa and back. Evidently, he thought the risk was not too great: if stopped by the Chinese, their interpreters would not detect that his fellow traveller had an accent and only a full strip search would reveal that he was not a real Tibetan.

Being a nomad and born in the saddle, it did not occur to Lozang to enquire whether Jeremy could ride. Where Lozang was raised, boys learned to sit on a horse almost as soon as they could walk. Fortunately, Jeremy had been taught to ride as a small boy when in Lhasa and had continued to practise his equestrian skills during his adolescence in England. He was an accomplished horseman.

From Tezpur the way into Tibet lay up the Brahmaputra valley, across the snow capped Himalayas and then along the Tsangpo valley to Lhasa. It was a well trodden trade route, known to caravan masters for centuries.

∽✦∾

Aten, the Khamba horseman, rode into the copse lying just beyond the precincts of Lhasa, made his way into the yard of one of the adjacent buildings and dismounted. Some lamas rushed out to meet him, taking the bridle of his horse.

"Om mani padme hum!" they chanted.

"Om mani padme hum!" came the reply.

Meaning *"Oh jewelled lotus!"*, this greeting, in common use amongst Tibetans, is in fact a mantra owing its origins more to Sanskrit than Tibetan.

Once inside the building Aten was offered traditional refreshments; a bowl of bod ja and some tsampa, that is, Tibetan tea with rancid yak butter and roasted barley grains.

He quickly explained the urgency and the needs of his

mission. Within a short while he was donning the red robes of a marriageable lama, not the yellow ones of chastity to which he could not pretend.

In the yard the lamas assembled, with Aten in their midst. Being taller than the local Lhasa men, he was given the staff of a banner to hold in the hope that it might divert the curious gaze of the sentries manning the cordon and so allow him to enter the Potala unnoticed.

With the sun sinking below the mountains in the west, the cortege of lamas set off for Lhasa. An icy cold wind lifted the dust on the road as they marched silently towards the checkpoint manned by two soldiers and an NCO. Their steady step seemed to defy any attempt to stop them and the NCO waved them on, giving them no more than a cursory glance. So far the deception had succeeded. Ahead lay the Potala Palace, the winter residence of the Dalai-lama and the hootooktoos to whom he had to deliver his message.

At the entrance to the palace, a lieutenant and a soldier came out of their sentry boxes and counted the number of lamas entering the palace. They had strict orders to maintain a precise tally of all comings and goings but no instructions about scrutinising or searching lamas. The cortege entered the gates of the palace without further ado.

Aten, showed little emotion at having reached his destination safely, so intent was he on his mission. He asked to see the hootooktoos and was led along a corridor and then down a long flight of steps deep into the basement of this fortress like building. A further walk along a corridor and he found himself in front of a heavy wooden door. Here he was told to wait.

Within minutes he was ushered into a bare, dimly lit

room where a number of hootooktoos, clad in yellow, were seated on mats in the lotus position. At the extreme end there was a large statue of Buddha. A pall of incense hung in the air.

"Om mani padme hum!"

"Om mani padme hum!"

He was not asked to sit but to deliver his message standing just inside the door. This he did in the Khamba dialect and strong voice typical of nomad people.

He told them that the main Chinese forces had penetrated so far west that the Tibetan army was behind their lines and that any retreat back to the Lhasa to defend the Potala would not be possible without a battle which they might lose. The Khamba irregulars were continuing their guerrilla raids on enemy convoys in mountain passes but could only delay the advance of General Tchou's reinforcements. If the fog were to clear, Chinese spotter MIGs would discover where both the Tibetan army and the Khamba irregulars were encamped. He concluded by saying that only certain mountain tracks to the south-east were free of enemy troops, this being a deferential suggestion to the high-priests that if the Dalai-lama were to escape and avoid abduction to Peking, it could only be via a mountain pass to the south-east.

His mission accomplished, he was thanked and escorted back to ground floor level, where he was given traditional hospitality comprising bod ja and tsampa. Having consumed these refreshments, he suddenly felt tired and asked for a mat to sleep on. There was no urgency now; he could await the orders of the hootooktoos just as well asleep as awake.

Once over the Himalayas and into Tibet, Lozang and Jeremy took the most direct route to Lhasa which lay along the left bank of the Tsangpo. Lozang proved adept at avoiding Chinese foot patrols and they journeyed without incident. When they were in sight of Lhasa they stopped to make camp and discuss what their next steps should be. Jeremy wanted to enter the city and attempt to find his childhood friends. He also wanted to gather material for the articles and book he was planning to write. Lozang believed that dressed as they were in the guise of Muslim caravan traders, he and Jeremy would arouse little suspicion from the Chinese sentries manning the cordon around the city. The Chinese were looking for Buddhists, and in particular a bespectacled twenty-four-year- old lama, not Muslims. They decided that the best time of day to approach the city would be at night. The flurries of snow in the air and the total lack of street lighting in Lhasa might make the visibility so bad as to allow them to slip past the sentries without being seen.

They settled down to await nightfall and the start of the most risky stage of their venture.

⚬⚬⚬

Colonel Tse-Wong of the Chinese army sat in General Ying's office listening to his superior's tirades against the Dalai-lama, the Tibetans and the fog which kept his MIG spotter planes grounded. The general had cause to be irate. No intelligence had emanated from any source about the precise location of the Tibetan irregulars, who for many months had been raiding Chinese supply convoys in the Cham province in the east of the country. An even greater source of anxiety was the whereabouts of the Dalai-lama himself. The best guess that military intelligence could offer was that the supreme spiritual leader was still in the Potala Palace. However, if that was so, why had a multitude of Tibetans, in excess of one hundred thousand, surrounded Norbulinka, the Dalai-lama's summer residence? They must surely know where their leader was hiding and had most likely assembled there to protect him from being kidnapped after it had been made public knowledge that the Dalai-lama had not accepted the general's invitation to take tea at his headquarters on 10th March.

Colonel Tse-Wong confined himself to echoing the general's words. He was supportive, even subservient without being servile. Well connected in Peking, he could afford to feel more relaxed than the general; Tibet was not his responsibility. Ostensibly he was an aide to the commander-in-chief of Chinese forces in Tibet, but his real function was known only to himself. He spoke Tibetan and had been a junior officer in the Chinese army which had first invaded the country in 1951. Without understanding why, Ying did not wholly trust Colonel Tse-Wong.

Having vented his ire, General Ying stood up and, followed by Colonel Tse-Wong, went to the window looking out onto the Potala. Chinese army headquarters were located in the city centre in a commandeered building whose windows had been glazed by army engineers to make them transparent. Most windows in the city were translucent; the panes being made of parchment which only allowed light to pass through. Ying observed the Potala as if awaiting some inspiration. He noticed the kites being flown by the boys of the neighbourhood and it suddenly occurred to him that they were of a different shape and colour from those flown on previous days. Perhaps this had a significance. He asked Tse-Wong what this change of shape and colour could mean. Tse-Wong told him that it was some holy day that was being celebrated and that no attention should be paid to it. The general appeared to accept this explanation but within himself he rapidly came to the conclusion that it was a kind of signal and that if only Tse-Wong could read it, the whereabouts of the Dalai-lama would be known.

∽👁👁👁∾

Aten awoke from a deep sleep. He opened his eyes and found himself on a mat on the floor of a dimly lit room. He recalled having asked for a place to sleep in the palace and quickly realised where he was and what he was doing there. However, one matter still perplexed him: what precisely had woken him? He had the impression of having been woken by a very loud bang. Soon he heard the sound of running feet and voices outside the room where he had been sleeping. He got up and opened the door.

As the heavy door swung open a throng of lamas in the corridor met his gaze. The enquiring look on his face begged an explanation for the commotion and he very soon learned what had occurred. His senses had not deceived him: there had been an explosion. A shell fired by a Chinese artillery unit had hit the south face of the building.

He speedily gathered his possessions and went to ask for orders from the hootooktoos. He was making his way along a corridor leading to an ante-chamber when he heard another explosion. He concluded that in view of the Dalai-lamas reluctance to take tea with the commander-in-chief of the Chinese occupying forces in Tibet, an order had been given to escalate the military offensive in the hope that this would persuade the lamas to deliver the supreme spiritual leader into Chinese hands.

⚬⚬⚬

A large caravan comprising more than a hundred camels and yaks was being mustered on the south side of Lhasa. Led mostly by Muslim traders, it was about to depart in a south-east direction, bound for India. The Chinese soldiers manning the checkpoint at the south gate had been observing it for some time. There was lots of movement but, as far as they could see, no co-ordinated activity. Yaks bearing loads seemed to come and go for no apparent reason. It was difficult to imagine how this heaving mass of beasts could ever be marshalled into the caravan of single file camels and yaks required to negotiate the narrow gorges and steep paths over the Himalayas. The spectacle of a caravan before departure was a mere distraction for the Chinese sentries; their task was to prevent the Dalai-lama and his bodyguards leaving the city.

⚬⚬⚬

Jeremy Boyd and his guide, Lozang, sneaked into the city midst a flurry of snow at two o'clock in the morning. They were not challenged and very likely were not even noticed by the sentries sheltering in their sentry boxes on that cold dark night.

Jeremy had told Lozang that he wished to find his childhood friends and hoped that they were still alive and well. Before leaving Tezpur he had started to search his memory in an attempt to recall their names. There was one who came readily to mind: Koido. However, try as he might, he could not recall his features and decided that the effort was pointless. Both he and Koido had surely changed in the intervening years as a result of their progression from childhood to adulthood. Lozang led Jeremy to a friend's house and advised him to stay there out of sight and off the streets. Having come this far, it would serve no purpose to be stopped by a Chinese patrol or even the dob-dob (local city police). This advice seemed sound and Jeremy, glad of an opportunity to rest, settled down to sleep on the mat his host, Tensing, had provided for him.

At about six in the morning, he was woken and invited to partake of a Tibetan breakfast with the family of Lozang's friend. This proved an entertaining experience. The younger children, obedient to strict Tibetan rules of courtesy, refrained from laughing aloud, but were clearly amused at the way Jeremy spoke Tibetan. His host's wife and eldest son gazed at him in wonderment. They offered him tea with rancid yak butter and aware that few non-Tibetans found such a beverage palatable, watched in rapt interest to see whether he would drink it. Jeremy took the bowl in both hands and raised it to his lips. The first sip seemed strange to him. He could not decide whether he wanted swallow it or turn away and spit it out onto the floor. Did it taste foul? he asked himself. Not wholly sure and not wishing to spurn the hospitality of his host, he swallowed it. At least it was warming, he thought and would stave off the hunger pangs he had been feeling since waking up. His hosts still continued to observe him furtively but when he took another sip, they adopted a different posture. It was as if he had passed some sort of test. He then began to eat the cereal set before him. What a curiosity; a westerner who spoke Tibetan with a strange accent and who could drink bod-ja, and eat tsampa.

On the streets day had dawned and Lozang, having finished his breakfast, said that it was time for him to start making enquiries on Jeremy's behalf. His friend, Tensing, urged caution; most Tibetans were reliable but some, like Probang, a prominent Lhasan citizen had already proved treacherous collaborators.

Whilst awaiting Lozang's return, a strange feeling of elation mingled with frustration came over Jeremy. He was in Lhasa for the first time in thirty years and yet, for his own safety, could not stroll about the streets. He asked Tensing if he might open a window and see the city that he was so curious about. Tensing agreed and led him to a small, second floor room on one side of which was a translucent parchment window. Telling Jeremy to kneel in front of the window, he opened it just enough to create an aperture through which his guest could look out. Although not a broad panorama, the scene that met Jeremy's gaze fascinated him. It awoke long forgotten memories: buildings with sloping roofs, whitewashed walls, and doors and window frames painted either red or yellow; two colours sacred in Tibetan eyes.

The cold Lhasan air started to fill the room and after a few minutes, Tensing, with a gentle hand on his guest's shoulder, said it was time to close the window and rejoin the other members of the family. In a state of mild euphoria and trying to recollect moments of contentment in what had been a happy childhood, Jeremy followed his host downstairs and sat by the stove in deep contemplation.

Lozang returned to Tensing's house at about midday. He did not have any encouraging news for Jeremy despite his efforts. He admitted to feeling hindered by the need for discretion. It would expose his friend, Tensing, to persecution and even execution if the Chinese or their spies had the least inkling that a westerner was hiding in Tensing's house. The determination of the occupying Chinese forces to capture the Dalai-lama and repress the revolt which was smouldering had already led them to commit acts of brutality in the city.

Feeling disappointed, Jeremy joined Lozang and his host's family for a bowl of bod-ja and some tsampa. During the course of this meal, he was party to a conversation, the gist of which he understood although some of it escaped him. Tensing's eldest son and some other boys were to be entrusted with a mission, whose purpose was not clear but which was of great importance. They were to leave the city limits just before sunset and would not be back till long after midnight.

It was half an hour before sunset when Tensing's teenage son and four of his friends ambled slowly towards the Chinese soldiers manning the checkpoint at the north-west gate. They seemed aimless as they passed the sentry boxes, chatting amongst themselves, each kicking a small object in front of him. The sentries did not challenge them; they were just boys playing some sort of a game and not the Dalai-lama, who was always accompanied by his bodyguard of twenty-five armed elite Tibetan soldiers.

Once beyond the cordon, the boys continued to stroll,

apparently aimlessly, in the direction of the trees lining the road half a mile outside the city. They disappeared from sight once they reached the trees. It was here, where the guards could not see them, that they sprang into life and began their work. Each took the horseshoe he had been kicking in front of him and bending down as if to touch his toes, used it to make an indentation in the dust such that the tail end pointed in the direction from which they had come. This they did diligently and earnestly, walking backwards away from Lhasa, judging the spaces between the indentations to match the stride of a cantering horse.

They continued fulfilling this arduous mission for more than two hours, straightening their backs from time to time and scanning the horizon as they did so. They wanted to be sure that they were not being observed. At approximately two miles distance from the city, at the site of a rocky outcrop, they left the road and directed the run of the horseshoe indentations towards a steep rock face, being careful from that point on to obliterate their own footprints. A hundred yards or so from the road they found themselves hard against an almost vertical wall of rock and pocketing their horseshoes, proceeded to climb upwards leaving the horseshoe tracks below them. Once they had reached a ledge one hundred and fifty feet above the ground, they then followed a mountain path back to a road on the west side of the city. Despite the darkness, it was an easy climb for them; they were Tibetans and knew every nook and cranny.

CALLED

TWO

⁂

General Ying had ordered a triple cordon to be placed around the Indian Consulate, ostensibly to protect its diplomatic personnel from the unrest that was brewing in the capital city. The invitation to take tea at Chinese army headquarters had been widely construed as an inept attempt to abduct the Dalai-lama and had given rise to open hostility amongst the Tibetans. However, it was clear to all that the triple cordon was ordered for other reasons.

The Chinese radio monitoring station set up in Lhasa to intercept signals that might be sent from subversives to governments and media in the west was constantly manned and proving effective in locating spies. However, it could do nothing to prevent messages being passed to Indian diplomats for onward transmission and so the general had placed a cordon around the consulate effectively impeding both entry to and exit from the premises. This risk apart, there was the remote possibility that the Dalai-lama might seek asylum in the consulate hoping to govern his people from within Lhasa but beyond the reach of the occupying forces; the cordon would deter the Supreme Deity from attempting such a manoeuvre.

Just before midnight Colonel Tse-Wong, on foot and

accompanied by a lieutenant, two sergeants and ten men marched up to the Indian Consulate. He answered with the correct password when challenged by one of the sentries, and giving orders for the sergeants and men to reinforce the guard, he and the lieutenant started to walk around the perimeter wall as if to inspect the security of the cordon. When out of sight of the sentries, he told the lieutenant to wait for him and challenge anybody who might approach. He advanced a few steps in the pitch black darkness and then, placing his hand on the wall and feeling his way along, came upon a small recess in which there was a door. He pushed the door, found it open and entered. There, a member of the consulate staff led him into an outbuilding in the grounds and showed him into a room at the end of a short corridor. As the door closed behind him he became aware of the heavily incense laden air and the presence of a man dressed in the robes of a high priest.

"Om mani padme hum! " came the customary greeting from a hootooktoo seated on a mat in the lotus position.

"Om mani padme hum!" said the colonel in Tibetan.

He sat down on a mat near the door and began to observe the hootooktoo in front of him. A silence ensued. After a minute the colonel announced that he had seen the kites being flown in the vicinity of Chinese army headquarters and that he was there in response to this signal to attend a meeting with the hootooktoo on the neutral territory of the Indian Consulate.

For a minute and more the two men sat scrutinising each other as if trying to detect some sign of treachery. Evidently satisfied with each other's bona fides, they began their meeting.

Forty minutes later having concluded his business with the hootooktoo, the colonel was shown the way back to the small door in the perimeter wall through which he had entered. Once on the other side of this door, he felt his way forward through the darkness to rejoin his men. Still giving the impression that his mission had been to inspect the perimeter security, he, together with the lieutenant and his platoon, returned to their quarters.

❧

Just before one o'clock in the morning Tensing's son returned home to inform his father that the mission had been accomplished. He and his friends had covered the north-west road with horseshoe tracks for approximately two miles and then had dumped the horseshoes in a fissure in the rocks a mile to the west of the city limits. This was an astute manoeuvre. On their return from their mission, they were stopped by a Chinese foot patrol and asked what they were doing so late at night outside the city limits. They told the interpreter that they had been scattering paper horses as a gesture to help the pilgrims travelling on foot. They added that it was the custom to make paper horses and scatter them to the four winds for those unable to ride to Lhasa. This explanation met with scorn on the part of the officer leading the patrol and he sent them on their way without further ado. It might have proved detrimental to their plan had they been found with the horseshoes.

As soon as he had heard this report from his son, Tensing slipped out onto the street on an urgent errand.

❧

Jeremy Boyd, asleep on a mat in Tensing's house, awoke suddenly to find that both Tensing and Lozang were standing over him, calling his name and shaking him by the shoulder. Tensing had just returned from his errand and appeared agitated. He told his guest that streets of Lhasa, although calm at present, could soon erupt in violence and that there would be reprisals on the part of the Chinese towards Tibetan civilians. This meant that he, Jeremy, could not stay in his house any longer. It would be dangerous for both Tensing's family and Jeremy. To this Lozang added his word: he, Lozang had decided to leave Lhasa and return to Tezpur in India and if Jeremy wanted Lozang to guide him back over the border, they must start immediately. He also insisted that Jeremy burn his notebook and pencil in Tensing's stove.

Lozang's dictate required no detailed explanation to justify it. Jeremy had been filling in the hours spent in Tensing's house by writing up his notes on the journey across the Himalayas and his impressions of life in a Tibetan family. If stopped by a Chinese patrol, the notebook would be found and their claim to be uninvolved caravan drovers would not be believed. They would be arrested and suffer the fate of all spies. Reluctantly, Jeremy conceded and the notebook, followed by the pencil, was devoured by the flames in the family stove. He would have to rely on his memory to write his articles and book.

⟨✺⟩

Five minutes before three o'clock at the north-west gate of the city the cold was intense and the night darker than usual. Crouching in their sentry boxes, more asleep than awake, the soldiers manning the picket were not aware that thirty men on horses were concealed behind the corner of a building, awaiting a signal from their leader to gallop through the checkpoint, out of the city in the direction of the trees lining the road about half a mile away; the very place where a few hours before Tensing's son and friends had started their task of making horseshoe indentations in the dust.

The signal given, the riders spurred their horses and rushed past the check point before the Chinese sentries could un-sling their rifles. Some shots were fired but too late; they had escaped without the Chinese even being able to count or identify them. The junior officer commanding that part of the cordon was stricken with panic. He dare not give the order to follow on foot because that would leave the checkpoint unmanned. Moreover, it would be impossible to catch horses. However, to admit that he had allowed an unknown number of riders to escape the city would mean a severe reprimand at least. After agonising over the decision he decided that he had no alternative but to inform his superior officer.

In the meantime, the horsemen, having reached the cover of the trees, searched for the place where the horseshoe tracks began. There, they dismounted and began to lay at right angles to the road, rugs they had brought with them. They laid them end to end, forming a path leading away from the road, over the dust and towards hard rocky ground some hundred feet away. They then led their horses along this carpeted path onto the hard ground where horse tracks are impossible to detect. The last man was entrusted with the task of picking up the rugs and loading them onto his mount as he went. This ruse and the horseshoe tracks laid by the boys a few hours before, meant that anybody following them later would not be aware that the fugitive riders had left the road. The whole manoeuvre took only a few minutes and was completed well before the duty officer even had the time to call out the guard in hot pursuit.

Being careful to remove any droppings, the riders climbed back into their saddles and rode off keeping to the rocky ground. About three miles from the road, content with their night's exploit, they scattered, fanning out in all directions in the quadrant north to west. Only two horsemen set off in an easterly direction : Lozang and Jeremy.

The telephone rang in General Ying's private quarters. He rose from his bed and stumbled over the cold floor to answer it. Still not quite awake. he fumbled with the handset. "Ying", he said in a gruff voice.

The news from headquarters that a band of horsemen, perhaps thirty in number, had broken through the checkpoint at the north-west gate made him incandescent with rage. He became calmer when he was told that Major Cheung with a company of men in three transport vehicles was in hot pursuit. He replaced the handset and began to wonder. Could the intelligence service be mistaken about the location of the Dalai-lama? Had he just broken through the cordon? Cheung was a competent officer and would soon catch the fugitive riders and make a full report.

The major climbed into the cab of the first of three transport vehicles. It had taken him less than five minutes to respond to the emergency call informing him about the breach of security at the north-west gate. A band of horsemen, perhaps thirty, had stormed through the check point. Was the Dalai-lama among them? It was his task to find out and make a report direct to General Ying.

The transport vehicles carrying the major's squad of elite troops gathered speed as they left the check-point behind them on the road out of the city. Cheung did not stop to speak to the junior officer commanding the checkpoint. It would be the general's task to reprimand him. For the moment the focus must be on catching the riders who had escaped the cordon.

As they approached the trees lining the road half a mile from the checkpoint, a thought occurred to Cheung. Suddenly he ordered his driver to stop. The whole convoy came to a halt. After a brief pause for reflection, he ordered his lieutenant to take a torch and light the way ahead, being sure to follow the horseshoe tracks in the dust and note if any of them left the road. Cheung knew how wily the Tibetans could be. If some of them had left the road and the rest continued to gallop on as a decoy, he wanted to know precisely where they had split up. As the convoy rolled forward, its tyre tracks would obliterate all trace of horseshoes in the dust, making the task of following any break-away group lengthy and tedious. Pleased that he had had the wit to take such a precaution, he sat back in the cab of the first transport as it glided gently forward in first gear. Catching the Dalai-lama was a prime objective and the general would not excuse any blunders.

The three transports had been tracking the horsemen for about an hour when the convoy came to a rocky outcrop and a bend in the road. Here the lieutenant seemed to hesitate for a minute or so and then, raising his hand, signalled to the driver in the first transport vehicle to stop. Cheung got out of the cab and went to see what had seized the lieutenant's attention. He looked down at the ground beneath him. Illuminated in the light of the lieutenant's torch he could see quite plainly that the riders had taken advantage of the bend in order to leave the road. Cheung felt a glow of satisfaction. His caution was justified. If he and his squad of elite troops had sped along the road in hot pursuit they would have missed the point where the Tibetan riders had decided to deviate from the well worn route. Knowing that horses must be watered, Cheung felt sure that it would only be a matter of time before he caught up with the riders and perhaps, even the Dalai-lama. He ordered the lieutenant to continue following the trail and climbed back into the cab of the first transport. The convoy moved slowly forward.

The young officer carrying his torch stumbled forward over the more uneven ground bordering the road. The horseshoe indentations seemed to lead on to a black bulking rock face. He raised his hand and the driver in the first vehicle stopped. Torch in hand he carefully picked his way forward until, to his consternation, he found himself against a steep rock face. Perplexed, he retraced his steps in the hope of locating the spot where the horses might have made a sharp turn. There was no sharp turn. The horseshoe tracks led right up to the sheer rock face and disappeared into it. Cheung's mood of jubilation rapidly dissipated. Without getting out of the cab, he could see what had caused the lieutenant to stop. The horses and riders had vanished into thin air. They had not climbed the sheer rock face, nor had they turned to the right or the left.

He began to think. If they had doubled back to regain the road, where could they have gone after that? They must be hiding somewhere.

Whilst in the midst of these deliberations, Cheung noticed that a sergeant in the last vehicle was allowing his men to stretch their legs and perform a natural bodily function. He bellowed orders that nobody was to put a foot on the ground without permission. The only hope that he had of finding which way the riders had gone was the dusty tracks on the road; a whole squad of men trampling the ground would make the task impossible.

Fearful of what the general would say when he made his report, he and the lieutenant edged their way back to the road in the hope of finding some clue as to how a band of thirty riders and horses could have vanished. He shared General Ying's dislike of Tibet and the hoaxes its people played on his troops. He had served his country well in Korea and had earned his major's commission. Would all that he had striven to achieve now be cancelled out in this land of mysticism and telepathy?

⟨≈≈≈⟩

General Ying was more and more convinved that the Dalai-lama had escaped from Lhasa but wondered how he had managed to slip past the pickets surrounding the Potala and then elude the numerous patrols throughout the city. Could he have been one of the horsemen who had galloped through the checkpoint at the north-west gate? There were good grounds to suppose that he had flown and was hiding in his summer residence at Norbulinka. Reports had reached Chinese Army Headquarters that an estimated two hundred thousand lamas, peasants and Lhasa citizens were thronging the roads and fields around Norbulinka. The only reason for such a multitude was to prevent the arrest of their leader whom they knew to be in his summer residence.

Ying was curious about Colonel Tse-Wong, a Peking appointee, not wholly under his command and so free to function independently. Although overtly sharing the general's opinion that the Dalai-lama was at Norbulinka, the colonel had taken on the task of inspecting and motivating the troops manning the checkpoints in and around the capital city.

The colonel had started his rounds early in the morning and was nearing the end of his tour of inspection, when at about five minutes before nine o'clock, he, a lieutenant and a squad of elite troops marched up to a checkpoint on the south face of the Potala Palace at the base of the Marpo Ri, the 600 foot hill upon which the palace stands. The lieutenant and other ranks stood to attention whilst the colonel spoke to the junior officer and men manning the picket. His questions were challenging and all eyes and ears were focused on the colonel. It was then that something occurred which, had it been seen by the sentries, would have caused the alarm to be raised.

At some hundred yards distance from the picket, just as a prayer bell sounded, three figures, probably Muslim caravan drovers, emerged from a crevice in the rock face and within less than twenty seconds were mingling with a team of yaks lumbering their way along a road leading past the Potala and out of the city. The average Tibetan bull yak, at its neck, stands at least six foot six above the ground. This feature of these beasts of burden enabled even the tallest of the three figures to conceal himself behind the team without having to stoop. Apart from the colonel none of the Chinese military personnel could have seem them; they were all standing to attention and facing the wrong way. It is not even sure that the colonel saw them, so busy was he haranguing the troops.

The team of yaks and their drovers continued on their path towards a checkpoint in the south-east of the city. The colonel concluded his inspection of the picket at the base of the Marpo Ri and marched off behind the yaks, overtaking them and reaching the checkpoint before they did.

The junior lieutenant manning this picket, intimidated by the colonel's presence and aware of what had occurred the night before when thirty or more horsemen had broken through the cordon, resolved to be meticulous in the search of the yaks and their drovers. He asked what goods were being transported and was told that they were carrying tea bricks and churpi, a sort yak cheese. At this point the colonel intervened, complaining that he had much to do and would not wait whilst pointless questions were being asked. The junior officer with a wave of the hand signalled to his sergeant to allow the yaks and drovers to pass.

Colonel Tse-Wong explained that General Ying was sure that the Dalai-lama would never leave the Potala without his retinue of twenty five armed elite soldiers and that at this phase in the occupation the general did not want to antagonise caravan drovers, who were obviously Muslim and not Buddhist devotees of the Dalai-lama. Delivering this admonishment seemed to relax Tse-Wong and he, followed by his men, returned to Chinese Army HQ.

The team of yaks were by that time a hundred yards

outside the city limits, making their way to the muster point for the caravan preparing to cross the Himalayas into India. The junior officer entered the details of the stop-and-search into his log book, sure that he had not committed the same blunder as his fellow officer the night before at the north-west gate.

⚭

The news that Major Cheung had failed to apprehend the runaway horsemen and had even lost their tracks, plunged General Ying into a state of depression. He was too anxious to be angry. He knew that Cheung was a competent officer and that if he reported that the tracks led up to a steep rock face, it must be so. A band of thirty or so horsemen could not disappear into thin air and the only explanation was that once again, the Tibetans had succeeded in hoaxing the Chinese army. He feared what would be said in Peking if the whole truth were known. Feeling morose, he sat in his office looking out onto the Potala Palace, a bowl of steaming hot green tea in front of him.

Slowly, as his thoughts settled, he began to think that the Tibetans had staged the breakout for one of two reasons: either they wanted to remove the Dalai-lama from Lhasa or create the impression that they had removed him. The latter thesis was the most credible in Ying's opinion. The two hundred thousand Tibetans currently surrounding Norbulinka were part of the subterfuge intended to persuade him that the supreme spiritual leader of the Tibetan people was at Norbulunka not in Lhasa. The pickets surrounding the palace formed such a tight cordon that the supreme spiritual leader and his retinue would not be able to leave without being stopped. He could not have been one of the thirty horsemen who had succeeded in galloping through a checkpoint in the hours of darkness.

As the General thought this through, he decided that provisionally laid plans to storm the Potala Palace at midday should be put into operation. The prospect of undertaking decisive action dispelled his anxiety. He would outmanoeuvre the hootooktoos. What would it matter in Peking that some riders had broken through a cordon in the middle of the night, he, General Ying, would soon be holding the Dalai lama in custody and the mission would be a success.

With a smile on his face, he reached for the telephone to give his orders.

⟨≋⟩

At about ten in the morning, the Chinese soldiers manning the checkpoint at the south-east gate became aware that something was happening in the middle of that heaving mass of yaks and camels that they had been observing for some days just outside the city limits. They knew it was a caravan being mustered but had been bewildered by the apparently aimless comings and goings of teams of yaks and occasionally a few camels. Only this morning another team had joined the hundred or so other beasts of burden already trampling the ground midst a cloud of dust. It all seemed so purposeless.

Suddenly there appeared to be a surge of co-ordinated activity. A column had formed and was moving slowly away from the city towards the south-east. As the beasts came into line one by one and trudged towards the horizon, the

Chinese soldiers watched, aware that soon there would be nothing left to look at apart from the mountains. A sense of loss came over them; observing the strange activities of a mustering caravan did make the long hours on duty in the cold more bearable.

By eleven o'clock the caravan was almost out of sight and with it, the three drovers who had slipped out from the crevice in the rock face. They were bound for the Himalayas.

∽◠◡◠◡◠◡◠

At midday whistles sounded all around the Marpo Ri and a thousand Chinese elite troops rushed up the paths leading to the Potala Palace. They forced the doors with explosives and battering rams and surged into the Supreme Deity's residence. Carefully briefed and well disciplined, they had a clear idea of their objective; to seize the Dalai-lama alive. They had been shown film of him and were sure that close up they would recognise him. However, they had been warned that the wily Tibetans might try to disguise their leader and dress other lamas to look like him. It would be a mission requiring much judgement and perhaps a little brutality to persuade obstinate lamas to co-operate and refrain from pointless deception.

They stormed into the thousand and more rooms for which the palace is famous, starting in the basement and progressing up to the roof-top terrace. Any Tibetan who even vaguely resembled the Dalai-lama was escorted out of the building into waiting troop transport vehicles. The others were unceremoniously bludgeoned or even bayoneted.

General Ying in his office looking out onto the Potala, observed the execution of his plan, well aware that the whole operation would last for some time and that after the arrest of all lamas resembling the Supreme Deity, his military police interrogators would need to spend hours, if not days, sifting the haul of Dalai-lama look-alikes. He had arranged for a camp to be constructed on waste land near the Potala and would assist in the interrogation process as soon as the first phase of the operation had been completed. General Ying felt decidedly optimistic; he was in control of the situation. The Tibetans would learn that it was no easy matter to dupe a general in the army of the People's Republic of China.

⌘

Tibet occupies a plateau situated at altitudes over 10 000 feet above sea level and is located between 30 and 40 degrees north. Because of its altitude it has a climate as cold as Northern Europe, but because of its latitude it resembles Africa in its hours of daylight. There is no substantial difference between the length of day in winter and summer and the duration of sunrise and sunset is noticeably shorter than in northern latitudes. Travellers in the wilds of the country are aware that darkness can descend on them suddenly and not possessing artificial light, their practice is to stop just before sunset, using the last rays of the sun as illumination in order to make camp for the night.

Having left Lhasa at ten o'clock that morning, the caravan with the three escapees from the Potala, journeyed southward towards the Himalayas. The sun was minutes away from disappearing below the horizon when it came to a halt near the confluence of the Kyi and Tsangpo rivers. The drovers unsaddled their mounts and offloaded the packs from their yaks and camels and then corralled these beasts in the time honoured manner with a peg in the ground and a tether around the forelegs. After which, in the last rays of the sun, they kindled a fire using dry grass and horse manure. Once ablaze, they stoked it with yak dung, a widely used fuel in Tibet. It was then time for bod ja, tsampa and ritual story telling

In the morning the sun rose as suddenly as it had set. Pale and wan, filtered by the fog, it illuminated the drovers camp and revealed the presence of forty or so Khamba horsemen who had spent the night on the banks of the Tsangpo half a mile away. Two of the Khambas rode over to parley with the drovers.

Om mani padme hum!

Om mani padme hum!

This traditional greeting was exchanged between each and every individual. They seemed unabashed by its repetitiveness. The fire smouldered and bod ja and tsampa were made ready for all.

As the drovers began to reload the packs onto their yaks and camels preparatory to moving on, the Khambas, together with the three mysterious escapees from the Potala, returned to their camp and with the other Khambas rode off to a place where the Tsangpo may be forded. There they crossed the river and following the right bank, started their journey eastwards and upwards into the mountains, in the direction of China and the Indian province of Assam.

ᘓᗕᗕᗕ

General Ying, in anticipation of success in his quest to seize the Dalai-lama and succumbing to pressure from

Peking, sent a signal to his superiors to the effect that he had the Dalai-lama in custody. As a military exercise, the storming of the Potala had been perfectly executed and there were good grounds to suppose that the Supreme Deity was amongst the haul of lamas transported to the makeshift camp on the waste land adjacent to the palace. However, as the hours passed and the interrogations continued, the stark reality became apparent: the Dalai-lama was not amongst the prisoners. General Ying trusted his military police but, in view of the importance of capturing the Dalai-lama, he had also participated in scrutinising the line-up of dozens of lamas, dressed, some in yellow, some in red. The interrogation of the most likely prisoners had been conducted by Colonel Tse-Wong, which led the general to assume that the colonel's real function, as designated by Peking, was to employ his command of Tibetan and knowledge of the culture to good end, namely, to identify the Dalai-lama and then persuade him that China's occupation of his country was in the best interests of the Tibetan people. This thought reassured Ying who had felt threatened by Tse-Wong ever since he had been posted to Lhasa.

Despite withholding food and drink and other forms of coercion, not one of the detainees would reveal the least detail about their Kundun, and none of them resembled him: they were too old, too tall or lacking in some essential feature peculiar to the supreme deity.

Full of anxiety, Ying received a telephone call from the colonel commanding the pickets around Norbulinka. The great multitude of Tibetans besieging the summer residence, no doubt to prevent the abduction of the reincarnated Buddha, had started to disperse. The day before he had estimated their number to be in excess of two hundred thousand but, when the sun rose, it was plain to see that they had dwindled to less than one hundred and fifty thousand and that those who remained were striking camp. Thoroughly bewildered, Ying ordered the colonel to storm the summer residence and arrest all Tibetans in it. Anyone vaguely resembling the supreme deity was to be transported to the camp in Lhasa under triple armed escort.

Ying now regretted having sent a despatch to Peking confirming that the Dalai-lama was his prisoner. Elation turned to despair as he realised that once again he had been duped by the Tibetans, a people so primitive that they had no wheeled transport, no glass, no electricity or any other device. He rejected the very notion of telepathy. Nevertheless, without radio or telephone they seemed able to communicate with each other over long distances. Chinese telecommunications engineers could intercept radio and telephone messages, patrols could seize letters being carried by couriers but nobody in the Chinese army had a telepathy badge.

His mood changed when the air-force officer commanding the airfield informed him that improved visibility over the landing strip would allow for one reconnaissance sortie to be carried out. It was essential to seize the opportunity, because the fog was forecast to thicken during the night. The general ordered a radial sweep of the whole Lhasa region. Any column of horses, camels or yaks was to be reported.

CRNNO

The forty or so Khambas, together with the three escapees from the Potala, one of whom was the six foot tall

Aten, believed themselves to be behind General Tchou's main contingents as they journeyed south-eastward, following narrow mountain tracks. They felt sure that they would encounter no hostile forces, nor be spotted from the air in the mountain fog which was thickening as they climbed.

Meanwhile, the caravan with which they had parted company at the confluence of the Kyi and Tsangpo rivers early in the morning, was proceeding south-eastward along a well trodden trading route in the open plain of the Tsangpo river.

General Ying's orders to scramble two squadrons of MIGs came as welcome relief to the Chinese pilots. Glad to be airborne after days spent on the ground, they flew outwards from Lhasa airfield in a radial pattern, similar to the spokes on a bicycle wheel. In the southern sector covering the Kyi and Tsangpo plain, the fog had cleared as far the foothills of the Himalayas, where it appeared as dense as ever. It was inevitable that one or more of the Chinese MIG pilots would spot the caravan. How can one conceal one hundred and fifty beasts of burden and their drovers raising clouds of dust as they lumber along?

A simple radio message from one pilot and then another alerted the officer commanding the air force unit that a long column was making its way towards the frontier with India. Within minutes General Ying was informed about the column's co-ordinates and direction of travel. Thereafter, the general's intelligence officers speedily identified it as the caravan that had been observed mustering days before the storming of the Potala.

Although unable to imagine how and in what circumstances the fugitive Dalai-lama might have joined the caravan, the general was sure that its purpose was not trade but to smuggle the Supreme Deity out of Tibet. With the co-operation of General Tchou, whose main contingents were not far from the reported position of the caravan, he might still capture his quarry, so avoiding the disgrace of failure and the harsh regime of a labour camp. He sent a radio signal to Tchou advising him to intercept the caravan and apprehend the Dalai-lama.

As he settled to drink a bowl of green tea Ying mused that Colonel Tse-Wong, Peking's special envoy, was mistaken about the Dalai- lama. The Supreme Deity would condescend to mingle with lowly drovers, even Muslim drovers and must have left the Potala Palace without an escort. All of which Tse-Wong had stated were beneath the dignity of the His Holiness, the Kundun. Reassured by these thoughts, Ying leant back in his chair and started to doze.

⦿

Jeremy Boyd riding alongside his guide, Lozang, had but one preoccupation; to return to India safely. His curiosity about the country where he had spent some of his childhood had dissipated. Hunger, dehydration, fatigue and perhaps a touch of mountain sickness aggravated by anxiety, were making him averse to all things Tibetan. It was not Shangri-la he was leaving behind; what he was fleeing from was anything but utopia on the roof of the world. Moreover, he had detected something in Lozang's demeanour which indicated a change of attitude. It was as if he had been appraised of some disturbing news, with which his innermost soul was striving to come to terms.

They had been riding eastward since having broken through the cordon at the north west gate the night before and were both glad to stop and make camp. A bowl of bod-ja and a little tsampa revived Jeremy's flagging spirit. Despite this, he avoided conversation with his guide, remaining plunged deep in his own thoughts. Ahead lay a long journey, first in the direction of China and then over the Himalayas to India. Although Lozang believed that General Tchou's reinforcements were already to the west of them, there was no way of being sure. Capture was still a possibility.

At daybreak they set off again, climbing higher and higher into the mountains. Despite having slept during the night, Jeremy felt weary; every movement required more effort than usual. As if in a daze he followed Lozang along a winding mountain track which led south-eastwards in the direction of India.

Suddenly Lozang reined his horse and beckoned Jeremy to do the same. Hardly had he responded when he became aware of two horsemen, one on either side of him, and a rifle pointed at his chest.

A tall Khamba told them to dismount and follow him on foot. With armed Khambas to the left, right and behind, he felt it wiser to be compliant. Daring to glance to his left, he saw that Lozang was also a prisoner.

Now on foot, with a Khamba rifle in his back, Jeremy stumbled forward. An experienced horseman, he had been able to sit upright in the saddle despite his fatigue, but walking over the uneven rocky surface beneath his feet was almost beyond the limits of his physical strength. He teetered along behind the Khamba horseman leading the procession. Fifty yards away, concealed behind an immense boulder, was a narrow cleft in the steep mountain face. The Khamba dismounted and pushed Jeremy and Lozang into the cleft. They found themselves in a tight, twisting passage. Khamba rifles in their backs goaded them forward. There was insufficient headroom and they were obliged to stoop as they made their way to the end of the passage into what appeared to be a dimly lit cave. Jeremy's eyes struggled to penetrate the gloom.

༄༅༅

General Tchou received Ying's signal and immediately dispatched a company of soldiers, commanded by a major, to intercept the caravan and seize the fugitive Dalai-lama. The honour of capturing the supreme deity was to fall to him. He would succeed where Ying had failed abysmally. A summons to return to Peking and a court martial would be Ying's fate

In less than two hours' march, the major and his troops came across the caravan. A huge cloud of dust pinpointed it on the horizon. As they drew near, they fired shots over the heads of the drovers signalling them to stop. Once alongside the muster of yaks and camels, the major's men set about executing their orders with unmistakeable glee. They lined the drovers up at gunpoint and began the process of identifying who amongst them might be the Dalai-lama.

They had no photograph but knew the supreme deity to be in his mid-twenties, small in stature and clean shaven. Their glee turned to frustration as they realised that the men before them were Katchis, that is, Kashmiri Muslims. Typical of their race, the drovers had bushy black beards and were dark skinned. Their clothing and calloused working hands betrayed their religion and profession. In no respect did they resemble the Dalai-lama, who like all Tibetan men, would have a sparse beard and pale yellow skin. Moreover, being a spiritual leader, his hands would be smooth and unaccustomed to hard manual work.

The Chinese soldiers snatched at the drovers' turbans and tugged at their beards, fit to provoke retaliation had it not been for the rifles pointed at them. None of the men looked like the Kundun, the supreme spiritual leader. Their hands were rough, their beards black, their skin dark and they were all too tall and too old. The Katchi drovers, outnumbered and outgunned, were powerless to resist the indignities meted out to them by Tchou's soldiers. Nevertheless, they seethed with anger at such treatment.

The Katchi people had migrated from their native Kashmir centuries before in order to escape the atrocities of a tyrannical despot. Initially they had married local women but as generation succeeded generation, they began to isolate themselves and form a separate community within the host population. They built a mosque in Lhasa, married only amongst themselves and raised their children as Muslims, scorning the religious practices of the Buddhists. Although the indigenous Tibetans thought them impious, they respected them for their wealth. Without question, the best shops in Lhasa were owned by Katchis. They dealt in gold and silver and imported goods from India, such as scissors, knives and fine fabrics. In order facilitate this trade with India, a former Dalai-lama had granted the Katchis special rights, including armed escorts for caravans journeying to and from the frontier high in the Himalayas. Lowly Tibetans, when passing them in the streets of Lhasa would indicate their respect by sticking out their tongues and rubbing their right ears. The Katchis jealously guarded their privileged position and dreaded the prospect of Tibet being governed by the Chinese instead of His Holiness, the Dalai-lama.

Angry and frustrated at not finding the supreme spiritual leader, the Chinese soldiers began a search of the caravan itself. They wrenched the bundles off the yaks and camels and ripped them open with their bayonets in the hope of finding something incriminating, such as weapons and ammunition. All they found was tea bricks and churpi.

THREE

As Jeremy's eyes grew accustomed to the gloom, he could see that at the end of what was quite a long cave, there was a large assembly of lamas and a small group of hootooktoos. The Khambas forced him and Lozang to the ground whilst one of them, whom they all called Aten, went to deliver his report to the hootooktoos seated in the lotus position just above the lamas. A long discussion followed during which the hootooktoos glanced from time to time at Jeremy and Lozang couched on the ground. It was clear to Jeremy that their fate was being decided.

The discussion ended, Aten strode back across the floor of the cave in his heavy boots and khaki robes. Standing over his captives, the Khamba spoke to his companions in words which Jeremy did not wholly understand. Although the dialect was unfamiliar, it was obvious that he was giving them instructions from the hootooktoos. Feeling weary and dazed, Jeremy thought it better not to ask Lozang for an explanation and lay still, glad to have an opportunity to rest and not exert himself. He started to doze.

A Khamba boot in his buttocks woke him. Then a voice from somewhere above and behind told him to stand. Once on his feet he became aware of Lozang standing to his left.

A hand applied to the back pushed him forward and he and Lozang began to move deeper into the cave. Jeremy still feeling tired, was relieved to think that it was a hand and no longer a rifle muzzle that had pushed him forward. They were not prisoners of the Chinese, he told himself and might even be in humane hands, despite the abrupt manners of their captors.

At the far end of the cave, lit only by yak butter lamps, a rock cast a flickering shadow on to a young man seated in the lotus position. He was dressed in traditional Tibetan gho and kera, a knee-length tunic tied around the waist with a band. On either side of him stood Tibetan soldiers and Khambas. A voice asked them who they were. Lozang took the initiative and spoke first, explaining that they had come from Lhasa and were on their way to India. The question was repeated and a hand touched Jeremy on the shoulder.

It was Jeremy's turn to explain himself. He spoke in faltering Tibetan, stammering in places. He was not at all sure that his words were coherent or comprehensible. Disconcerted and dismayed at this poor performance in what he considered to be his second mother tongue, he fell silent, having only spoken a few words. Weariness combined with anxiety had robbed him of his fluency.

The stern faces staring at him seemed to soften. A pause followed. Then the young man wearing traditional gho and kera and sitting in the lotus position, spoke to him.

"Do you speak English?

"Yes"

"Where do you come from?"

"I'm British, living in India."

"Where are you going to?"

"I'm going to India."

"With Lozang as your guide?"

"Yes"

The young man nodded and whispered some inaudible words to the hootooktoos.

Jeremy then felt a gentle hand lead him away back to the cave entrance. Lozang followed a few paces behind.

Here Aten beckoned to them and pointed to the way out of the cave. Once outside in the cold air, he told them to mount their horses and wait for the order to move off. As they were settling in their saddles Lozang told Jeremy in a whisper to ask no questions about what had just occurred. He was to see nothing, hear nothing and say nothing. Above all, he should not even think about the young man dressed in Tibetan gho and kera. Jeremy glad to be alive and back on his horse had no wish to jeopardise their safety and assured Lozang that he would keep his eyes on the road and his tongue still.

The Khambas, lamas and hootooktoos came out of the cave and mounted their horses. With very little ceremony the cavalcade then moved off. In the van were a dozen Khambas, with Jeremy and Lozang in their midst. Then came the lamas, some Tibetan soldiers, the Hootooktoos and in the rear some more Khambas. They entered a narrow tree-lined gorge leading upwards, in the direction of the snowy mountain tops. Although still light-headed, Jeremy started to feel better and less anxious. The column was climbing and so must be wending its way towards a col, a low point between two snow capped peaks from which they could descend into India. If his captors had wanted to kill him and Lozang, they could have done so already.

Remembering Lozang's advice not to think about what had occurred, he focused his attention on remaining in the saddle as his horse picked its way over the rough ground.

The trees and other vegetation on the sides of the gorge were thinning out when, without ado and as if by a pre-arranged signal, the column halted to make camp for the night. They all dismounted and set about lighting fires to make bod ja and tsampa. As he observed these preparations, Jeremy became aware that Lozang and he were still being closely watched but not guarded as they had been when first taken prisoner.

Soon the fires began to glow. Their warmth and light comforted Jeremy. He reflected on what he knew and what Lozang had told him in conversation about the art of fire making in Tibet. The most commonly used fuel is dried, compressed dung, the best source of which is sheep and goats. Their tarry droppings burn without smoke and can raise an iron bar to red hot heat within twenty minutes. Camel, yak and cow dung are less efficient; they burn brightly but never hot enough for purposes other than cooking. In contrast, horse manure is only fit for kindling; it burns quickly, giving off much smoke and too little heat. The major difference between these traditional nomadic fuels and horse manure lies in the fact that sheep, goats, camels, yaks and cows are all ruminants; horses are not. Horses do not chew the cud nor do they have a second stomach. Therefore their fodder does not undergo so intense a processing.

Traditional Tibetan food is eaten out of a bowl which, when not in use, is carried in a bag suspended from the belt. With a true sense of gratitude Jeremy saw his bowl filled with bod ja and tsampa and crouched on the ground to enjoy this simple but much needed nourishment. Feeling more secure, if not totally at ease, he stretched out on the ground and fell asleep.

❦

General Ying sat in his office morosely contemplating the wall whilst Colonel Tse-Wong stood looking out of the window. News had just reached Lhasa Army HQ that Tchou's troops, despite an exhaustive search, had not found anybody evenly vaguely resembling the Supreme Deity amongst the caravan drovers. It irked the general to think that after such long years of service to his country, his career should end in ignominy because of a failure to succeed in what had been an impossible mission. He acknowledged only one mistake: he had been too eager to inform Peking that the Dalai-lama was already in custody. He should have resisted the temptation to win approval from his superiors by telling them what they wanted hear. It would have been wiser to wait for confirmation that the Dalai-lama was one of those arrested in the Potala and Norbulinka raids. Colonel Tse-Wong, without consulting him, had already sent a full report to Peking on the interrogation of all prisoners taken in the storming of the two residences. Army chiefs and the government were now aware that His Holiness was still at large and that he, Ying, had blundered. The more he thought about it, the more he loathed Tibet and everything Tibetan.

The caravan train lumbering towards the Himalayas had been his last hope of redeeming himself. The reconnaissance MiGs had not reported any other convoy in which his quarry might be travelling. Therefore, according to his reasoning, only one possibility remained. The fugitive Supreme

GEORGE RENTON

Deity, despite his rank had joined the caravan somehow, somewhere, and at that very moment, was seated astride a yak on his way to India. He would hardly have taken any other road. The news that the Dalai-lama was not with the caravan disguised as one of the drovers plunged Ying into despair. Where else could he be?

He looked up at Tse-Wong as if asking for inspiration. The colonel, stiffening his facial muscles to conceal the smug satisfaction he felt, reminded the general that from the outset he had said that the Supreme Deity would never stoop to travelling with Muslim drovers. He must still be in the city, Tse-Wong added.

Ying's only reply was that a house-to-house search in Lhasa might result in casualties and the alienation of those Tibetans willing to collaborate with the Chinese government. The truth was that Ying was so demoralised that he had lost the will to command. He did not relish his recall to Peking but was beginning to feel that it would be a relief.

⚬⚭⚬

Aten sat on a rock with a bowl of bod ja and tsampa and watched the two prisoners he and his Khambas had captured the day before. One was a Lhasan refugee living in India with his family who had returned to his native land as a guide. The other was a curious individual; a Tibetan speaking foreigner. Neither of them were Chinese and did not appear to sympathise with the occupying forces. Nevertheless, they could be spies or saboteurs able jeopardise the whole mission at this most crucial stage. His preference would have been to keep them prisoner in the cave until such times as they could do no harm. However, orders had been given that they should be allowed to continue their journey to India under close supervision to ensure that they did not stray and fall into enemy hands. That was the reason why they were riding in the van surrounded by elite Khambas.

The sun was just rising and it was time for the column to get under way. Ahead lay the Pra-po, a narrow part of the gorge so strewn with huge boulders that it was impassable to horses. Here they would have to dismount and continue on foot. Even for fit men it would be difficult to clamber over or ease past the massive rocky obstructions. More difficult still would be squeezing themselves through a series of narrow clefts in the rock. At six foot tall Aten would experience more problems than some of the Lhasan lamas. However, there was no doubt that the effort would be worthwhile. Beyond the rocky obstructions there would be fresh mounts waiting for them. Thereafter the gorge continued upward to the col and the frontier with India.

The most obvious alternative route over the mountains was the Jelep-la pass at 14 000 feet above sea level. Like all other well trodden passes it was certain to be patrolled by hundreds of Chinese troops ready to pounce on anybody moving along it in either direction. However, Chinese commanders were unlikely to know about the Pra-po gorge and even if they did, they would rightly conclude that it was impossible get past the boulders on horseback. The gamble was that they would not believe it feasible to arrange for horses to be waiting on the upper side of the obstruction: without horses it would be impractical, even undignified, for the Dalai-lama and members of his party to continue the journey over the mountains.

Once at the col, they would rendezvous with lamas waiting for them on the Indian side of the frontier and Aten's mission would be accomplished. He and his men would then return to their native province of Kham in order to continue the struggle against the Chinese invaders. For his own safety the Kundun, their Supreme Deity was on his way into exile in India. One day he might return. They would be ready to greet him.

⁂

Western heads-of-state, through their spy networks, were fully aware of events in Lhasa and Tibet. They knew that the Dalai-lama was being manoeuvred into an impossible position and that he was making a bid for freedom, but they had no notion of how he planned to escape. Where he might try to escape to was obvious. India was the only choice. All around Tibet, to the east, north and west lay provinces of China. Accordingly they started to lobby Indian diplomats in the major capitals of the world in an attempt to persuade the Indian government to offer him asylum on humanitarian grounds. What was at issue was not merely a matter of opening the frontier to a refugee. India's relations with China were at a delicate stage in view of a looming border dispute and allowing so prominent an opponent of Chinese expansionism to seek refuge in India might escalate the tension. However, the Indian government was aware that in some influential Chinese politburo circles, there was tacit acquiescence to the exile of the Dalai-lama in India. The real source of contention was Aksai Chin in the Jammu Kashmir province and the discovery of a road built by the Chinese in what was claimed as Indian territory.

On the 3rd April 1959 Pandit Jawaharla Nehru, the Indian Prime Minister announced to the world that the Indian Parliament had granted asylum to His Holiness the Dalai-lama.

⟨❧⟩

Colonel Tse-Wong leant back in Ying's chair and took stock of the situation. Ying had been recalled to Peking and he, Tse-Wong, had been appointed acting commander of the Lhasa garrison pending the arrival of a replacement for the general. The world media were now agog with the news that the Dalai-lama had safely reached India. How he had eluded the Chinese army was a matter for speculation in all the capitals of the world, not least in Peking where Ying was facing a court martial for having allowed the Tibetan leader to escape.

Taking a sip of green tea he mused that had Ying succeeded, he, Tse-Wong, would have failed in his mission. The plan nearly went awry. Tchou's troops might have found their quarry had the MIGs located the caravan sooner. Instead they were too late and found only Muslim drovers transporting tea bricks and smelly cheese. Despite his familiarity with Tibetan culture, like most of his compatriots, Tse-Wong had an aversion to cheese.

The damage done to the Potala was slight compared with what the summer residence at Norbukinka had suffered. Indiscriminate shelling had reduced parts of it to rubble. The repair bill would be high, an inevitable consequence of Ying's ineptitude and failure to comprehend the essentials. Nevertheless, he played his part to perfection, albeit unwittingly.

Politburo members and their advisory committees in Peking were unable to reach unanimity on how to implement their long term plans for Tibet. They all agreed that the province was of such strategic importance for the future of the People's Republic of China that there was no alternative to governing it directly from Peking. However, opinions differed about what to do with the Dalai-lama, the spiritual leader of the country.

Whilst some favoured assassination and others exile, the majority believed it possible take him prisoner and exploit him as head of a puppet government. They argued that to kill the Supreme Deity would serve no purpose. Dalai-lamas, although bound by chastity to be childless did procreate in a strictly Tibetan Buddhist sense: reincarnation. Within two years of the death of a Kundun, a small boy would be found somewhere in a tiny village and this child would be endowed with the powers and office of the Supreme Deity. Slay one dragon and another will appear.

Likewise, exile would be counterproductive. The knowledge that the Kundun was alive, watching over his people from afar would prevent the Tibetans from settling into the new order. The thought that one day he might return would keep the fires of insurrection smouldering.

The only viable plan would be to maintain the Dalai-lama in the Potala as a titular leader. With a subtle mix of threats and promises, this young man might be cajoled into endorsing Chinese plans for development. Apart from China's strategic interests, the proposed reforms would be to the advantage of both peasant and city proletariat. The whole country was riddled with feudalistic practices which bolstered the lamas in their dominant position whilst denying the people the advantages of modern technology. There were 1892 different sorts of taxes, including a tax on ears, but no electricity, no wheeled transport and no telephone.

These were the arguments that were presented in favour of abducting the Dalai-lama. The majority approved and General Ying was given the order to seize the Supreme Deity, preferably without provoking a riot on streets of Lhasa. Colonel Tse-Wong, in contrast had secret orders to dialogue with the hootooktoos and facilitate the escape of General Ying's quarry. His orders came from the highest authority.

It was only ignorance of Tibet and the Tibetan people that allowed the majority to entertain the belief that the Dalai-lama would submit to political manipulation. Far from being putty in the hands of the Chinese governor, the likelihood was that despite his youth, the Supreme Deity would prove a very able politician, exploiting his native knowledge of the language and the culture to thwart Chinese plans.

In contrast a leader who chooses to go into exile has abandoned his people and leaves behind him dissent which can develop into schisms and disunity. In the absence of unity, an occupying force can establish its authority, unchallenged, save for sporadic rebellions. In time, the significance of the absent leader would wane and the next generation of adults, having spent their childhood under the rule of the new regime, would know nothing else and might even be hostile to the restoration of a feudal theocracy. This was the policy of the most influential clique in Peking, but for reasons of expediency they deemed it better not to promote it overtly. Hence the mission entrusted to Colonel

Tse-Wong, a man with an extensive knowledge of the Tibetan language and culture. If it were possible to succeed in facilitating the departure of the Dalai-lama from Tibet, whilst creating the impression that he had fled to avoid facing his responsibilities, Tse-Wong was the man to do it. General Ying, a good soldier, but lacking in imagination, was to be the stooge whose inept execution of his mission would reinforce the belief that the supreme spiritual leader had chosen exile when danger loomed.

With a profound feeling of contentment, the colonel settled deeper into his chair and started to doze.

∽◦◦◦◦◦◦◦◦∼

Once over the border and safe in India, Jeremy fell ill with a mild case of Shiga dysentery. Lozang found lodging for him at Towang monastery. Apart from his stomach pains, he was exhausted and needed to rest. In the meantime the column of lamas continued further down the valley of the Brahmaputra.

In eight days Jeremy was well enough to climb back into the saddle and he and Lozang made their way to Tezpur without incident. Arriving in Tezpur on 30th April, Jeremy learned that the Dalai-lama had escaped from Chinese occupied Tibet and had been granted asylum in India. Now recovered from the dysentery and the malaise he had suffered in the mountains, he began to recall the events of the past six weeks. It was a pity he had burnt his notebook with all his jottings. However, had they been stopped by the Chinese it would have been found and both he and Lozang would have been arrested as spies. He was sorry that circumstances had not allowed him to renew acquaintance with his childhood friends or visit the city in which he had spent some of his most formative years. All these thoughts aside, there remained a matter which perplexed him: Who was the English speaking young man he had met in the cave? Without doubt, the young man exercised great authority over the Khambas and the lamas. It was he who had given the order to allow him and Lozang to ride with the column. Could it be that he had met His Holiness the Dalai-lama and even ridden with him on his flight into exile?

Lozang had successfully accompanied Jeremy into and out of Tibet in the most difficult circumstances and payment for Lozang's services was now due. Feeling more than a mere contractual obligation, Jeremy withdrew from his bank the sum that had been agreed plus a generous bonus. At a farewell meeting he paid Lozang expressing sincere thanks and best wishes for the future.

Before taking leave of his guide, he asked the identity of the young man who had questioned them in the cave where the Khambas had held them prisoner. Was he the Dalai-lama?

Lozang merely smiled and repeated the advice he had whispered to Jeremy as they mounted their horses, closely watched by Aten: see nothing, hear nothing, say nothing and think nothing.

Om mani padme hum!
Om mani padme hum!

GEORGE RENTON

NOTES

In 1994 the Potala Palace was designated a World Heritage Site

In 2001 the Norbulinka residence was designated a World Heritage Site

Printed in the United States
by Baker & Taylor Publisher Services